3 - 3/20-2/23

D0252681

Pippa BY DESIGN

A STORY OF
BALLET AND COSTUMES

Pippa BY DESIGN

A STORY OF
BALLET AND COSTUMES

CLAUDIA LOGAN
ILLUSTRATED BY CHESLEY McLAREN

Frances Foster Books
Farrar Straus Giroux
New York

Farrar Straus Giroux Books for Young Readers
An imprint of Macmillan Children's Publishing Group, LLC
120 Broadway, New York, NY 10271

Printed in China by RR Donnelley Asia Printing Solutions Ltd.,
Dongguan City, Guangdong Province
Designed by Cassie Gonzales
First edition, 2019
1   3   5   7   9   10   8   6   4   2

mackids.com

Library of Congress Cataloging-in-Publication Data

Names: Logan, Claudia, author. | McLaren, Chesley, illustrator.
Title: Pippa by design / Claudia Logan ; [illustrated by Chesley McLaren].
Description: First edition. | New York : Farrar, Straus and Giroux, 2019. |
    Summary: While her sister studies ballet at Toronto's National Ballet of
    Canada, the head of the wardrobe department encourages eleven-year-old
    Pippa's interest in fashion and costume design.
Identifiers: LCCN 2019000364 | ISBN 9780374359560 (hardcover)
Subjects: | CYAC: Ballet—Fiction. | Costume—Fiction. | Costume
    design—Fiction. | Fashion design—Fiction. | Family life—
    Canada—Fiction. | Toronto (Ont.)—Fiction. | Canada—Fiction.
Classification: LCC PZ7.L82765 Pip 2019 | DDC [Fic]—dc23
LC record available at https://lccn.loc.gov/2019000364

Our books may be purchased in bulk for promotional, educational, or business use.
Please contact your local bookseller or the Macmillan Corporate and
Premium Sales Department at (800) 221-7945 ext. 5442 or by email at
MacmillanSpecialMarkets@macmillan.com.

There's an old friend
I once heard say
Something that touched my heart
And it began this way . . .
—Sam Cooke

For Lissa, who made the impossible possible
Lois, who does the impossible
And Abby, who reminds me of what is still possible

A STORY OF
BALLET AND COSTUMES

WEDNESDAY

Me: Pippa. Eleven years old. Not an interesting age or number, unless you are doing multiplication tables, in which case it's handy.

Current Location: the great city of Toronto. Dad calls it the New York of Canada, only much, much smaller.

Actual Location: cold, hard, greenish linoleum floor outside Studio C of the National Ballet of Canada.

Why: The National Ballet of Canada has its own company of professional dancers and a school where students can take ballet classes.

One of those students is my older sister, Verity, which means Mom has to bring her to class, which means I have to tag along. Every. Single. Wednesday. Sigh.

Escape Plan: none. Mom has a very strict no-complaining rule.

Upside: the vending machine and . . .
MY SKETCHBOOK.

I like to draw fashion: ball gowns, outfits, and shoes. Mom thought it would be a good idea for me to get a head start on my homework while we waited for Verity. I said using the time to draw was an even better idea, especially since it was Mom who enrolled me in art classes at Le Studio in the first place.

On the first day, our teacher, Ms. Von der Bleek, gave each of us our own sketchbook, because "art is always waiting to be discovered." What I discovered was how much I liked drawing in a sketchbook.

I didn't exactly keep this information to myself, which turned out to be a good move because . . .

I have a grandmother who lives in London. Her birthday presents can be a little hit or miss, but this one came from a store with three names and a bunch of hyphens. The box was an incredible shade of blue, which I was told is the store's signature color. I figured

even if the gift was a bust, I could use the box, but when I opened it, there was a sketchbook with a real leather cover in the same signature blue and thick, cream-colored paper inside.

I called my grandmother right away to say how much I loved my present. She is a stickler for spelling, speaking clearly, and manners, especially in the thank-you department. I knew I still had to write a "proper note," but this time I didn't even mind.

"I heard you were taking an art class, so I thought this might be just the thing for you," she said. "It is sooo important to have an interest and the right accessories."

I agreed with the part about the right accessories, but the "interests" part was a touchy subject.

Unlike Verity, who sticks with everything she has ever tried, I don't have the best track record in that department. A few of my *uninterests* (a word my grandmother would say is incorrect):

Theater Lights Group

Looooong rehearsals so I could develop stage presence and learn to PROJECT my voice—all so the entire audience could hear me say one line: "Nobody new has been in these parts for years." (Pronounced *yars*.)

Soccer Stars

I am not much of a soccer fan, but it is the game of choice at my school. Every kid belongs to at least two teams, and Mom was worried I would feel left out. I did not feel left out, as cleats are not my thing. Or kicking.

Or running up and down a long field. I gave it two weeks.
Two very long weeks.

Tenley Aquatics

Swimming in freezing-cold water in the middle of winter. Add in a bathing cap, the green mold in the locker room showers, and the little kids from the next class running around, screaming . . . Need I say more?

Anyway, back to Le Studio. Ms. Von der Bleek took us on a mini field trip to draw some of "nature's wonders," which were conveniently located in a nearby park. The inconvenient part was when we found out that, along with our sketchbooks and drawing tools, we each had to lug one of those wooden easels with the legs that stick out. When we started grumbling, Ms. Von der Bleek said, "All great artists suffer for their art."

I hope all great artists get distracted, too, because even though I knew I was supposed to sketch the ficus tree, I ended up drawing a lady sitting near the tree who was wearing the most incredible hat.

I was worried Ms. Von der Bleek would be mad that I didn't follow her directions, so I explained to her that a hat with a brim that wide should count as one of nature's wonders.

She just said, "Follow your muse," which was a good thing since Mom would not have been "amused" if this class turned out to be another bomb.

When Ms. Von der Bleek found out my sister was in ballet class, she told me that this was an opportunity to draw inspiration from the dance world in the tradition of great artists like Édouard Manet and Henri Matisse.

"What if Edgar Degas had been forced to work on a dull little worksheet from school instead of creating his paintings and sculptures? There would be no *Dancers Tying Shoes, Ballet Dancers in the Wings, Ballet Rehearsal on Stage, Dressed Dancer at Rest, Little Dancer, Two Ballet Dancers, Three Dancers in an Exercise Hall . . .*"

And now we can add *Girl in Hallway with Sketchbook.*

It was getting close to the time when the classes turn over. Grown-ups were sitting in chairs waiting for their kids, while students in teal, violet, and blue leotards clustered outside the studios.

In ballet school, all the dancers have to wear a "uniform": black tights and slippers and a leotard in the color of your level.

Verity is in level four and wears a black-colored leotard with cap sleeves.

All of a sudden there was a loud ruckus from Studio C. The door opened, and the ruckus turned out to be Verity and her two friends, Enid and Noelle, jumping up and down and talking at the same time. It took a few minutes, but Mom finally got a complete sentence out of Verity: "We got picked to be in *Sleeping Beauty*!"

Oh boy. Verity is the kind of person who always gets picked. If one kid is

going to read a poem in front of the school, you can bet it will be Verity. At Emma Blum's wildlife-themed birthday party, Nature Guy even chose Verity to be his assistant instead of the birthday girl and hold the snake.

Verity is good at a lot of things, but ballet is her absolute passion. I feel sorry for anyone who ever gets stuck in an elevator with her, because she can barely let five minutes go by without sharing something she knows from the world of ballet.

Verity has tickets to see every single performance by the National Ballet of Canada, so I knew one of the ballets they were going to perform this spring was *The Sleeping Beauty*. What I didn't know was how Verity managed to outdo herself by getting picked.

"Oh my goodness!" said Mom. "I didn't realize they chose students to perform with the company."

When it comes to ballet-ology, Verity's only rival is Encyclopedia Enid, who wasted no time in telling us, "There are a hundred and ninety parts in *Sleeping Beauty*. The company dancers play all the principal and important roles, but there are some smaller parts given to students in the ballet school."

"It's easier to get picked if you're a boy," said Noelle, pointing one foot and sliding it along the floor in the shape of a fan.

I knew that boys took separate classes from the girls,

but I didn't know why that made it easier for them to get picked.

Enid saw that I looked confused. "It's just that because there are so many more girls than boys taking ballet, they have a better chance of getting picked for a male part."

"You still haven't told us your parts," said Mom.

"Don't tell me you're Sleeping Beauty?" I asked Verity.

"Oh no, not Sleeping Beauty," said Verity, shaking her head and looking shocked that I could even suggest such a thing. "And she's called *Princess Aurora* in the ballet, not Sleeping Beauty."

"Only a principal dancer gets to dance the part of Princess Aurora," said Noelle, gliding down the hall. "In fact, there is more than one dancer for each lead role since there are so many performances."

If there was a part for a broom, Noelle would be a shoo-in.

Enid filled in the gaps. "A ballet company is broken down into different ranks, with the principal dancers at the top. They get the main parts and are the stars. Next are the soloists, who—well—perform solos and understudy for the principal dancers in case one of them gets sick."

Verity interrupted Enid. "There's the *coryphées*, or first artists, who are a group of about six dancers. They have big parts but aren't stars." She used a fancy French accent so it sounded like she was saying *kaw-ree-fey*.

Not ready to give up as the official spokesperson, Enid swung back with "And at the bottom is the *corps de ballet*, which is the biggest group of dancers. The name is French for *body of the ballet*." Enid showed off her French accent, too, pronouncing *corps* like *kors*.

I was beginning to wish I hadn't asked anything.

Noelle swooshed in to add, "Don't forget character parts."

"A character dancer helps tell the story by acting through mime," said Enid.

"So did you get a character part?" I asked.

"No," said Verity. "Those parts go to senior dancers who are semiretired."

Noelle, worn out from dusting the hallway with her feet, flung herself to the floor. "Then there are the storybook characters, like Little Red Riding Hood and Puss in Boots, who appear during the wedding scene between Princess Aurora and Prince Florimund. That's when everyone dances."

"Are you Little Red Riding Hood?" asked Mom.

At this rate, we'd spend the night going through all one hundred and ninety parts. So I said, "If none of you are stars or soloists or first artists or dancers who mime or fairy-tale characters who go to a wedding, then WHAT ARE YOU?"

"We're supernumeraries," said Verity.

"That's fantastic," said Mom. "But what is that exactly?"

"It's what you call all the extra people in a scene," explained Verity. "We'll be performing with the entire company. Those dancers had to audition, but we were lucky, because our teacher recommended us."

"We get to be in the court scenes and the wedding scene," said Noelle. "But the supers—that's us—really do more standing and moving than dancing."

"But we'll be onstage and we have to go to rehearsals since it's a REAL PERFORMANCE. And not everyone got picked," said Verity.

"Well, I think it's super that the three of you are supers," said Mom. "Right, Pippa?"

"Superduper," I said flatly. "Now can we go?"

My fifth-grade teacher, Mr. Greenberg, likes to use the word *hullaballoo* when

the whole class starts talking at once. So I can say there was quite a hullabaloo when Mom gave Enid and Noelle a ride back with us. But the real hullabaloo happened when we got home and I didn't have my sketchbook.

I pleaded with Mom to take me back to the National Ballet, but she was trying to make dinner while Verity was standing on one leg, reading the rehearsal schedule and waving the forms she needed to get signed.

"Sorry, Pippa, but it's nearly dinnertime and you both have homework to do," Mom said. "Verity, why don't you write the rehearsal dates on the calendar, and I'll sign the forms later."

"The performances are from June twelfth to June twenty-second," said Verity, flipping the calendar pages. "And it's mid-March right now, so there are thirteen weeks till opening night.

"The week before we open is tech week," she continued importantly, "and we have rehearsals every day that week."

Mom always says she can only concentrate on one thing at a time, and right then a chicken was getting all of her attention.

"The company dancers rehearse every day"—Verity didn't seem to care if anyone was listening or not—"for hours and hours. But my rehearsals are mostly on class days and some weekends. I guess that's because they know we have school and stuff."

I wanted to say that "standing and moving," even if it is on a stage, doesn't require a lot of practice, but that would only lead to one of Verity's and my "skirmishes," as Mom calls them. Using a confident voice, I said, "I guess we know who and what's important around here, and it's not my sketchbook."

Verity turned around from writing on the calendar, and I was sure she would say that I was being a drama queen, but she surprised me.

"Mom, we really could go back and look for Pippa's

sketchbook. You wouldn't even have to get out of the car. I'll run inside with her."

I looked at Mom, hoping she would change her mind, but she was busy poking a fork into some yams.

"Salt, butter," she mumbled to herself. "No, girls, I'm sorry. It won't be long until dinner, and we'll go right after school tomorrow. Besides, the building is probably locked by now."

At dinner, when Verity and Mom were telling Dad about *Sleeping Beauty*, no one even noticed that I barely ate any of the chicken or mushed-up yams, which were clearly more important to Mom than a sketchbook that came in a box with a signature color.

Before I went to bed, I poked my head into Verity's room.

"Thanks for trying," I said.

"Sorry it didn't work," she said. "Don't worry. You'll find it tomorrow."

"What if it's gone forever?" I wailed. I am often told that I go right to the worst-case scenario.

"It's probably right where you left it, in the hallway," said Verity. "Why would anyone take someone else's sketchbook?"

For once I wanted Verity to be right.

THIS IS WHAT A WORST-CASE SCENARIO LOOKS LIKE

It starts with finding out that your sketchbook is NOT right where you left it.

Just as she promised, Mom picked us up after school and drove straight to the ballet building, and we went back to the hallway outside of Studio C.

A different group of parents were sitting on the chairs waiting for their kids, and when Mom explained that we were searching for my sketchbook, they popped up and looked underneath the seats.

WORST CASE SCENARIO

"despondent"

"MOROSE & INFURIATED"

I checked the floor where I'd been sitting, and Verity walked down to the end of the hallway.

"I told you we should've come back last night," I said to

Mom. "I hope that roast chicken was worth ruining my entire life."

When Mom gets mad she starts doing this weird thing with her jaw that looks exactly like a loggerhead turtle we once saw on vacation.

Verity noticed Mom "turtling" and realized nothing good was going to happen.

"Okay, here's what we'll do," she said. "Some of the classes will be ending soon. We can check the studios on this floor and the ones below and ask around. Mom can stay here and spread the word if anyone new walks by."

Mom nodded, and Verity grabbed my hand and pulled me down the hall to where a class of older dancers was getting out.

As far as detective work goes, this was pretty low on action. I was in charge of searching empty studios and hallways, which required more of a once-over since dance studios don't have anything except barres attached to the walls.

Meanwhile, Inspector Verity, wearing the determined expression she gets, asked every single person we saw if they had seen a blue sketchbook.

At one point I saw my sister, arms folded across her chest, grilling a group of little girls from one of the beginner classes.

"Are you absolutely sure?" Verity asked. "Think again, very carefully."

"We really didn't," a teeny, terrified ballerina in a pale-pink leotard replied.

Clutching their identical sparkly, black, patent-leather ballet bags, they took off as soon as they saw me come up to Verity.

"Should we haul them back to the station for more questioning?" I asked.

Verity looked a little embarrassed. "I just can't believe no one has seen your sketchbook."

It seemed that no one had. But more than one person had given us the same advice:

"No, sorry. Check with Ida."

"Haven't seen it. Did you ask Ida?"

"If anyone knows, it would be Ida. She's in charge of the lost-and-found."

This was probably great advice if you were someone who actually knew Ida.

It turns out that Verity did.

"I just remembered that Ida works at the reception desk in the lobby," said Verity, slapping her forehead. "I should have thought of her right away."

We reported back to Mom, who had lost her turtle jaw.

"Well, let's go find Ida," she said.

We found Ida at her desk, where she listened very patiently to my tale of woe.

"Let me check the lost-and-found," she said, lifting a big box onto her desk. Keys were clearly a popular item to lose; there were at least six sets. There was also a single shoe, a sad-looking mitten, and a sandwich wrapped in tinfoil.

"I think we'll toss this," Ida said, making a face at the old sandwich. Then she said, "Listen, hon: I know everyone. I'll put out an all-points bulletin for your sketchbook."

We walked back toward the car, and Verity said, "With Ida on the case, you'll get your sketchbook back."

Mom put her arm around me and said, "As the saying goes, all is not lost just yet."

ALL IS LOOKING PRETTY LOST

DIARY OF THE SEARCH AND RESCUE OPERATION

Friday: We drop by to see Ida. No sketchbook. No leads. No suspects. She suggests I make some signs and put them up over the weekend since the building will be open for rehearsals.

 Saturday: Dad helps me make signs and takes me to post them.

 Sunday: Nothing. I make bigger signs, Dad adds a reward, and we post those. We agree to only call Ida once a day so we won't bother her.

Monday: Unfortunately, we forgot to agree on who would call her. So I call Ida at recess. Mom calls Ida at lunch. Dad calls Ida in the afternoon. Three calls. No sketchbook.

Tuesday, March 19

We had to go to the ballet school on Tuesday so Verity could hand in all her forms to be in *Sleeping Beauty*. Mom and I stayed in the car. I didn't want to hear Ida tell me in her sad voice that my sketchbook was still missing.

When Verity came back, she was holding a pink booklet in her hand. She looked at me and shook her head.

REWARD

SKETCH
BOOK
MISSING
"URGENT"
"PLEASE CALL"
PIPPA

"What's that?" asked Mom.

"It's something we have to read," said Verity, "about *Sleeping Beauty*."

I stared out the window, blinking back tears. I was sick of hearing about *Sleeping Beauty* and grumpy from hoping every day that my sketchbook would turn up.

When we got home, we headed to the kitchen. Mom was making us a snack while Verity looked at her pink booklet and I sat on the counter, kicking my feet on the cupboard drawers below.

"Pippa, please stop that," said Mom. "I know you're upset."

"Tomorrow is the one-week anniversary of my sketchbook going missing," I said. "You were so sure I would have it back by now."

"I know a week feels like forever, but it's not. Anyway, Verity has class tomorrow, so you should plan to bring something to do with you."

"I'm not ready to go back there," I said. "It's too soon."

"I'm sorry, Pippa, but you still have to come with us."

"Can you bring the sketchbook from art class for now?" Verity suggested.

I shook my head. "We have to leave them with Ms. Von der Bleek."

"We could buy you a new one," Mom offered.

"No, thank you. I want my genuine blue-leather sketch-book," I said firmly.

"Verity, why don't you read to us about *Sleeping Beauty*?" Mom suggested.

Ugh. I didn't especially *want* to hear more about *Sleeping Beauty*, but I also didn't especially want to start my homework, either.

Everyone ignored my loud sigh, and Verity started reading.

"*Behind Beauty*, researched and written by National Ballet of Canada Archivist and Librarian Cece Coburn."

"What's an archivist?" I asked.

"It's someone who organizes and keeps documents, photographs, drawings, and anything else that tells you about an important event or person," explained Mom. "Usually they work in a library or a museum or a place that keeps special records."

"Is there a place like that at the ballet?" I asked.

"There's a library on the top floor," said Verity. "Now stop asking questions so I can read."

Dear Dancers:

You may already be familiar with the story of *The Sleeping Beauty*. It begins with the christening of the new baby princess, Aurora, followed sixteen years later by the curse that puts the entire kingdom to sleep for a hundred years, and then, finally, comes the arrival of a handsome prince, Florimund, whose kiss brings everyone back to life. Although the awoken princess is dressed in the style of his grandmother, Prince Florimund falls in love with her immediately. The ballet ends with a celebration for the marriage of Prince Florimund and Princess Aurora and their happily ever after.

But *Sleeping Beauty* is really two stories: one told through the ballet itself, and the other hidden in the sets and costumes. One story is a fairy tale, but the other is true.

Long, long ago the fairy tales we've come to know and love weren't written down. One seventeenth-century French writer, Charles Perrault, decided to write them down and make a book. Little did he know how famous the fairy tale of *Sleeping Beauty* would become or how it would eventually be adapted into a ballet.

Perrault was a writer and poet as well as a member of the king's royal court. It makes sense that his simple stories of enchantment, featuring kings and queens in grand palaces surrounded by important people wearing the finest and most expensive clothes, became wildly popular with a real-life king who lived in the grandest of palaces and whose court spent most of their days getting in and out of the finest clothing.

Who was this king, and where was this palace? Louis XIV was only four years old when he became the King of France in 1643, after the death of his father. Even back then, letting a four-year-old take charge of an entire country seemed like a terrible idea, so Louis had to wait until his twenty-third birthday to be crowned France's new monarch.

Like his father, Louis was very fond of ballet, and when he was fourteen, he danced the part of the sun god, Apollo, in *The Ballet of the Night.* His performance led to his nickname: the Sun King. Louis also had another name—one he gave to himself: *Louis le grand*, or Louis the Great. Whichever name he used, Louis XIV loved art, beauty, and extravagance and was determined to make France the center of culture, fashion, and fine taste in Europe.

He constructed a magnificent palace called Versailles, which was larger, grander, and more ornately decorated than any other royal residence the world had seen. From there, Louis not only ruled France but also ruled fashion. Nobles at Versailles followed a strict dress code set by the king, which required multiple changes of clothing throughout the day and night to keep up with the nonstop schedule of glittering balls, banquets, entertainment, and carriage rides.

Before Louis XIV, fashion meant wearing mostly black or dark-colored, stiff austere styles. "Sun King style" was loose, colorful, and heavy on trims, jewels, and beading. It was also time-consuming and expensive; these clothes required the purchase of costly, luxurious silks and satins, and wearers employed talented seamstresses and tailors to dress them in the latest fashions. Many of the styles showcased at Versailles became the foundation of ballet costumes.

When Louis XIV died in 1715, the throne was passed on to his great-grandson, Louis XV, who followed in his namesake's trendy footsteps. Both Louis number fourteen and Louis number fifteen would have been tickled right down to their fashionable breeches had they known that the styles they set would be used for a new ballet, *The Sleeping Beauty*, that was to debut at the Mariinsky Theatre in Saint Petersburg, Russia, in 1890.

Three people were behind this original production of *Sleeping Beauty*. They were:

Ivan Vsevolozhsky, a highly cultured man who was appointed director of the Russian Imperial Theatres in 1888. He was inspired to turn Perrault's fairy tale *Sleeping Beauty* into a ballet. While working for Russia's tsar, Alexander III, Vsevolozhsky designed the expensive and elaborate sets and costumes in the style of Louis XIV as a form of flattery, because Russia was trying to sign an economic agreement with France.

Marius Petipa, who began his career as a dancer and became Russia's chief ballet master in 1871. For the next thirty years, he produced classical ballets known as *"grands spectacles"* because of their dramatic themes and theatrical effects. Indeed, Petipa produced some of the great classical ballets we know today in this time frame, including *The Nutcracker* and, of course, *The Sleeping Beauty*. Nowadays, he is known as the "father of ballet."

Pyotr Ilyich Tchaikovsky, a composer and musician, understood what no composer had before, and that was how dancers needed to move onstage. Tchaikovsky and Petipa had a strong working relationship, with Tchaikovsky's music inspiring Petipa to choreograph with creativity, and vice versa, Petipa's skill in dance leading Tchaikovsky to new forms of musical composition.

———————— ⨍ ————————

Today *Sleeping Beauty* is performed all over the world by every major company, with many of the most famous dancers in the principal roles. It continues to use the same beautiful music, and although designers bring their own touch to the costumes and sets, they remain faithful to the style of Louis XIV and Louis XV. The sets and costumes are patterned after the reign of the Sun King. When you first try on your costume, look at it carefully and remember that you are wearing a piece of history.

"The end," said Verity.

"I had no idea there was so much history involved in this ballet," said Mom.

"It's a lot more interesting than reading about colonial people with scurvy," I said.

"That makes me think you might have some homework to do," Mom said.

"If I finish everything, can I please, please watch *Off the Rack* tonight?" I said.

"Only if you can tell me how to treat a nasty case of scurvy," said Mom.

Off the Rack is one of those reality-competition shows, and I never miss an episode because it's about fashion design. Dad, on the other hand, says it's a waste of time, yet he magically shows up whenever I'm trying to watch it. I say "trying" because he constantly asks questions and makes comments.

I finished my homework, ate dinner, turned on the TV, and, sure enough, Dad plopped down beside me on the couch.

"Is this that show *Squirm*, where they have to embarrass somcone?" he asked.

"Dad, cut it out. You know this is *Off the Rack*." I made a shushing noise as the host started talking.

"A fashion line only counts when it hits the racks. Our six fashion designers are competing for the opportunity to have their collection sold at retail giant THE Department Store. Who will win tonight's hanger, and who will go home with their garment bag?"

"So the garment bag is bad?" asked Dad.

"Dad, you watched this just last week. You know it's bad," I said.

"Now let's meet our panel of judges: Leticia Blum, head buyer for THE Department Store; Baskette, owner of the first invitation-only boutique, Address Unknown—"

"How can anyone run a business by inviting people to shop?" said Dad.

"—fashion show producer Austin Tornado; and Pinky Vogue, our sixteen-year-old social media star. And now let's hear from Baskette, who will tell us this week's designment."

"Dezzzigners, we all know that fashion rules, but this week you'll be getting your inspiration from some of history's fashion rulers," Baskette said. "When these ladies dressed to party, they really led the way. Each of you will be given an envelope with the name of one of these trailblazers as inspiration. Your designment is to mix up the past with the present and give us something that's fit to win."

In real life, the designers have a week to do research, sketch, buy fabric, and sew their designs, but we only get to see clips of everything. Most of the time someone is crying or bad-mouthing another designer, and everyone complains that

Marie Antoinette's skirts were notoriously long and full.
Marie Antoinette, Charles Thurston Thompson (1816–1868)

they haven't slept for days. Then everyone faces the judges in the lineup.

I knew right away that the designer who was assigned Marie Antoinette was in trouble. She presented a short silk slip dress.

When I pointed this out to Dad, he said, "It doesn't have to be exact, does it?"

"No, but it should have some details from that period," I said. "She could have added some ribbons and lace or gone crazy by making the dress really wide and full."

On the show, the judges were scribbling notes and

getting ready to deliver their comments about the slip dress. Then the host said, "Let's start with Austin Tornado. Your thoughts?"

Austin Tornado covered his eyes. "Honey, did you even visit a library or museum? Your dress wouldn't make it as underwear in the eighteenth century."

"Now let's see what Baskette has to say."

"Frankly, I'm stunned. Shocked. Flabbergasted. There's no visual reference point here. It's a travesty."

"Do you think it's a travesty, Leticia Blum?"

"Well, let's just say that the proportions of this dress are all wrong. Even going with a fuller skirt or some decorative trims would have helped make this more Marie Antoinette."

"Pinky Vogue, it's your turn to weigh in. Do you agree with your fellow judges?"

"I'm not sure what 'travesty' means, but I don't like this dress. The color is ick."

By the end of the show, three of the designers were sobbing, but Dad was impressed that my comments about the Marie Antoinette dress were the same as what the judges said.

"I told you it was an educational program," I said.

"Well, this time I must agree that you are off the hook for watching *Off the Rack*," said Dad.

HOPE, FEATHERS, AND A SURPRISE

One of the best things about school is that Mr. Greenberg likes to end each study unit with an activity that includes cake. In this case, that meant our class had a poet-tea, and we each had to come dressed as one of the poets we'd studied. I was Emily Dickinson, who wrote over a thousand poems mostly because she never left her house.

I recited a poem called "'Hope' is the thing with feathers."

Unfortunately, I never got to recite my own version:

"Hope" is the thing
To which you cling
When your family is tired
Of listening
To your woes about a blue sketchbook
Gone missing.

I tried to tell my sister about it in the car after school, but it was Wednesday and Verity always panics about being late for ballet class on Wednesdays. She rushed into the building with Mom scurrying after her. I was tired from spending most of the day as a poet who never got any fresh air, so I took my time by sloshing through puddles of dirty water.

Verity suddenly reappeared outside, yelling. I figured she'd left something in the car and wanted me to go get it.

"I can't hear you," I yelled back, feeling annoyed. It was only when I got closer that I understood what she was saying.

"Pippa, your sketchbook!"

I couldn't believe it. I ran inside, where Ida was standing behind the reception desk, holding it over her head. She handed it to me, and I hugged it close and gave it a little kiss.

"How wonderful!" said Mom.

"I'm so happy for you, Pippa," said Verity. "Ida, who found it?"

"Now *that* is a mystery," Ida replied. "It was on my desk when I came in this morning. But perhaps this will give us a clue," she said, lifting a long, flat box from behind her desk onto the counter next to it. The package was wrapped in shiny white paper and tied with ribbons and bows made from different fabrics.

An envelope with my name printed on it was taped on the lid. I opened it, took out the card, and read:

Dear Pippa,

I am returning your sketchbook along with a very big apology. I found it in the hallway one week ago and meant to leave it at the front desk for you. Unfortunately, I was leaving for a trip and forgot. You must have been so worried and upset, as it is clearly a very special book.

Now I have to add something else to my apology: I sneaked a peek inside. At first it was just to look for a name, but then I started to look at your drawings, and they are quite wonderful. I especially loved the silver gown.

You have every reason to be cross with me, and to try to make up for my forgetfulness, I've left you a surprise. Don't bend, fold, or tear it.

-Your Secret Admirer

"A secret admirer," said Mom. "Imagine that."

"Open the box," said Verity.

Meanwhile, Ida was telling anyone and everyone that my sketchbook had been returned by a secret admirer, and soon I was surrounded by a crowd of curious onlookers. I recognized some of the dancers, but there were also people who looked like they worked in offices and there was a delivery guy.

I opened the box, and there was something square and flat wrapped in layers of tissue paper.

I carefully pulled back the paper to find the most beautiful sketch I have ever seen in my life.

A little card lay at the bottom of the box. I picked it up and saw from the handwriting that it was from my secret admirer.

This sketch was drawn by my dear friend, Santo Loquasto. He's a very famous set and costume designer for the theater, movies, and, of course, the ballet. This sketch is from _The Tempest_, a ballet based on a play by Shakespeare. The character you see here is Ariel.

"Santo Loquasto," gasped one of the dancers. "He's a genius. Not to mention one of the busiest designers around."

Another dancer added, "I was in a ballet he worked on that had silver birch trees right on the stage."

"I was in a ballet set in a primitive world, and he had us wear temporary tattoos with art from the Aztecs and the Mayans," someone else chimed in.

Suddenly everyone was talking about Santo Loquasto:

". . . incredible details and imagination."

". . . says he's inspired by pattern, sculpture, and illusion."

". . . creates a visual experience for the audience by crafting a whole world onstage."

"You should come visit the library on the fourth floor," said a friendly-looking woman with blonde hair and tortoise-shell glasses. "I'll show you some photographs of his work."

Verity must have heard the "library" part, because she turned to the lady and asked, "Are you the archivist or librarian?"

"Why, yes," the lady said. "My name's Cece, and, actually, I'm the archivist *and* the librarian."

"Did you write *Behind Beauty*?" I asked. "We read it because my sister's in *Sleeping Beauty*."

"Well, in fact, I did," said Cece. "And I think one of my next projects will be to see what magazine and newspaper articles I can find so you can read about the amazing Mr. Loquasto. And congratulations on being in *Sleeping Beauty*," she added, nodding to Verity. "That's a big deal."

The little bubble of excitement that held all of us suddenly burst when Mom looked at her watch and announced the time.

"I have to get to class," Verity said in a panicky voice.

"Go ahead," said Mom. "We'll catch up with you."

I put the sketch back in the box and handed it to Mom to hold while I collected my backpack and the letter from my secret admirer.

"Take care of that sketch," said the birch-tree dancer.

"That's a piece of art you have there, honey. Treasure it," added another dancer in a purple crop top and leg warmers.

"Come visit the library," said a third girl.

"My sketchbook," I said, suddenly remembering that I'd put it down to read the letter from my secret admirer.

Ida handed the sketchbook to me.

"Here it is, safe and sound," she said. "And let's hope it stays that way."

I took the sketchbook and didn't let go of it until we were home.

A NICE IDEA

Guess the Secret Admirer became my new favorite game. Dad thought maybe it was Cece, and Mom wondered if it was one of the dancers.

"We don't know if your secret admirer is a he or a she," Verity pointed out.

By the weekend, with no new suspects, everyone was getting a little tired of playing. On Saturday morning, Mom suggested that it would be a nice idea to write a thank-you note to my secret admirer.

I agreed that it was a nice idea, but I also agreed that it

was a nice idea to go skating with my friends Hannah and Lucy and have hot chocolate afterward.

On Sunday, it seemed like a nice idea to see my friend Sylvie's new puppy.

"Did you write your thank-you note?" Mom asked at dinner.

"I thought about it a lot," I said, feeling squirmy.

"I take it that means no," said Dad.

After dinner, Mom handed me a box of stationary and pointed to the table where Verity was doing homework.

"How do I write to someone when I don't even know their name?" I asked.

"Just write 'Secret Admirer,'" said Verity.

"Do I still use 'dear' and capital letters for a secret admirer?"

"Yes and yes," said Mom.

"Should I say it's okay that they forgot to leave my sketchbook? Because it wasn't really okay, but the Santo Loquasto sketch is a pretty big apology."

"I think you answered your own question," said Dad.

"How am I supposed to deliver the letter if I can't mail it?" I asked.

"Leave it with Ida," said Verity.

"At this rate, it's going to take you a very long time to actually write this note," added Mom.

When I finished, I showed it to Verity.

"You said 'thank you' a lot," she said, "but it's fine."

Dear Secret Admirer,

Thank you so much for finding my sketchbook and returning it. I got it on Wednesday, when my sister had ballet class. The Santo Loquasto sketch is so beautiful.

I'm going to get it framed, and I want to know more about him. I even kept the ribbons and bows from the package.

I hope I get to meet you someday so I can thank you in person. I will be around the studio a lot because my sister just got cast in <u>Sleeping Beauty</u>.

I'm really happy to have my sketchbook back. Thank you again.

Love, Pippa

On Monday after school, Mom drove me to deliver my letter to Ida, and Verity came in with me. Ida was busy stuffing envelopes.

"Did you find out who Pippa's secret admirer is?" Verity asked.

"The mystery continues," she said, shaking her head.

"I want to leave a thank-you note," I explained. "But how will the person find it?"

Ida put down the envelope she was holding and thought for a moment. "Here's the thing," she said, pointing to the counter beside her desk. "This is where all the special deliveries, packages, and whatnot are left. Everyone always checks it, so it's the best place to put your note. I'll keep my eyes open to see who, if anyone, picks it up."

"Don't you wish you just knew?" asked Verity when we got back in the car.

"Mostly yes," I said. "But it's the most exciting thing that's ever happened to me, and once I find out . . ."

"You feel like everything will just be the same again," said Verity.

I nodded because I didn't want to say that when things went back to normal, she would still be Verity the star and I would just be me.

"Here's a mystery you can solve," said Mom. "Guess what you need to start when you get home?"

Verity and I looked at each other and rolled our eyes, because that was such a parent-y thing to say.

THE FOURTH FLOOR, OR
THE BEST-CASE SCENARIO

This week instead of dance class, Verity and all the dancers in the crowd scenes were being measured for their costumes. When we arrived at Studio C, a mob of students and parents were crowded around a tiny woman.

You could tell that she had been saying the same thing all day: "If you hear your name, please take the elevator to the fourth floor and go to the wardrobe department, where someone will take your measurements," she said.

Verity was in the first group that was called, along with Enid and Noelle.

"You come, too, Pippa," said Mom, and we all squished into the elevator with the other dancers.

The elevator opened onto a hallway cluttered with racks of jackets and tutus and boxes. Verity marched ahead with her I-am-in-charge face, followed closely by Enid and Noelle. The rest of the group trailed behind in little clusters.

I stopped to look at a long wall covered with framed drawings and sketches and watercolors of costumes from different performances.

Verity and the others stood in the doorway to the wardrobe department, where a woman with chopsticks in her hair was holding a clipboard.

"You three go right in. The lady in the purple shirt will help you," I heard her tell them.

"Are you coming, Pippa?" Mom called.

"In a minute," I said, looking at a sketch of a balloon skirt with crazy black-and-white patterns all over it.

"Okay," said Mom before disappearing through the door.

"What do you think of that sketch?" asked a voice.

The voice belonged to the lady with the chopsticks, who was suddenly standing beside me. She had friendly eyes behind a pair of red-framed glasses.

"It's really like a piece of art. Well . . . I guess all of these are," I said.

"You are quite right," she said. "They were all created by different costume designers."

"I wish I could draw like that," I said.

"Well, from what I've seen, I wouldn't be a bit surprised to see one of your sketches up here one day. Perhaps a silver gown . . ."

"What do you mean . . . ?" I asked, my voice trailing off as things started to click into place, like when you figure out which character in a mystery is guilty.

"I'm Marjory Fielding, head of the wardrobe department and your secret admirer."

Just then Mom came walking down the hall and everything became a jumble of "I can't believe it" and "we never would have guessed" and "thank you so much" and "how wonderful."

After we settled down, Marjory asked Mom if she could give me a tour of the wardrobe department. "I was thinking it might be a good experience for a future designer to spend her Wednesdays with us, if that's all right with you?"

"Oh, Mom, please," I said.

"Are you sure you aren't too busy?" said Mom, looking around at the horde of dancers waiting to be fitted.

"I'm very sure," said Marjory. "Pippa, you'll want to get out that fancy sketchbook of yours so you can take notes when you meet my crew."

And that was how my worst-case scenario became my best-case scenario.

Here are the many Whos of the wardrobe department:

The Who: MARJORY

Official Title: Wardrobe Supervisor

The Person Who: DOES EVERYTHING. She works with everyone to turn the designers' sketches into costumes that the dancers wear onstage. Plus she manages, schedules, budgets, orders materials, and deals with big and small problems.

Which Means: a lot of work with a lot of people. It can take two years to get a very big ballet ready. Sometimes production and wardrobe people are working on more than one ballet at the same time.

Always Says: "No two days are ever the same."

Fun Fact: When Marjory was little, she dressed her dog in costumes that she made herself.

Two Whos: RUTH AND CHRIS

Ruth's Official Title: Resident Cutter/Draper

Chris's Official Title: Resident Cutter/Tailor

Which Means: For a costume to have a shape, you need to cut and drape.

They are the architects and construction crew who build the costumes. They use their sharp minds and tools to cut and drape fabric into 3-D forms. There's an expression that says cutters and drapers must be able to "talk to the fabric" and understand how to work with it.

Chris and Ruth supervise a team of stitchers.

Things Get Tricky When: Sometimes a designer has an idea that won't work, so the Resident Cutters have to be what Ruth calls "a polite elephant" and explain in a nice way why a certain look can't be made or must be changed.

Fun Ruth Fact: She knows how to drive an eighteen-wheeler truck.

Fun Chris Fact: He is also a costume designer and draws the most beautiful sketches.

(I wonder if you can be the designer and the cutter for the same costume? What happens when the designer and the cutter have to talk? Do you switch from one side of the table to the other? Chris seems to be everywhere all at the same time, so I'm guessing he might be magic.)

Two More Whos: LILY AND LISA

Official Titles: Resident Stitchers

Which Means: *Stitcher* is the title for someone who takes the cut-up pieces of fabric and attaches them together to turn into costumes. Some of the sewing is done by machine, but the detail work and decorations can be very complicated and need to be sewn on by hand. All of the stitching needs to be done carefully and neatly so that the stitches don't show and so they're strong enough that the costume won't fall apart even when dancers are stretching their bodies in all directions.

What's All This About a First Hand?: It turns out that one of the stitchers is also called a "First Hand." I put one of mine up and said, "What's that?"

Here's the 411: The First Hand refers to the most experienced stitcher. That person is in charge of the other stitchers and assists the draper with pattern-cutting, fabric layout, and fitting of the dancers.

The First Hand isn't the only stitcher with a special title; Marjory told me that some stitchers are bodice experts, tutu experts, or even fabric experts. She also said that if I can remember everything I learned today, I will be a costume shop expert.

At dinner, Verity asked me how the costumes are made.

"Costumes are not 'made,'" I answered. "Wardrobe people call it *building a costume.*"

"You don't need to sound like the expert of the world," said Verity in a huffy voice. "You've only been there for one day."

"Why don't you explain what building a costume means?" said Mom, who could see where things were headed.

"Well," I said, enjoying the feeling of being an expert, "they call it 'building' because a costume has to last about thirty years—they are expensive and take a long time to design and build. One costume gets worn by many different dancers."

"Does that mean other people have worn *my* costume?" asked Verity, dropping her fork on her plate.

"This production does use some of the original costumes, but Marjory said some of them also have to be made—I mean *built*—so yours might be new," I said, then added, "Some of the old costumes also have to be altered so they fit the dancer in the new production perfectly."

Verity still looked nervous.

"Anyway," I continued, "every costume has a label sewn in it with the names of every dancer who wore it. *Real* dancers think it's good luck to wear the same costume another dancer wore, especially if the dancer was famous."

"Oh," muttered Verity.

I could tell she was torn between wanting to learn something interesting and wanting to get mad at me for saying "real dancers."

"Marjory says a costume has to help create the character and allow the dancer to move easily."

"It sounds like you learned a lot from just one afternoon," said Dad.

"It sounds like she's getting to be a fathead know-it-all," said Verity.

"It sounds like you might be jealous," I said, making a little face.

"It sounds like after dinner it's time for homework and bed and not another word from either of you," said Mom.

LANYARD WEDNESDAY

My first real day in the wardrobe department began with Ida looping a lanyard around my neck that had a special visitor card attached to it.

"Now you're official," said Ida. "Do you have your sketchbook?"

"In my backpack," I said, "and I promise not to lose it."

"Good. I don't think any of us could take it," said Ida.

When I arrived at the wardrobe department, I stopped in the doorway to admire the room. There were people looking at fabric laid out on long tables, working on sewing machines, and standing in front of mannequins. I wasn't sure where to go, but then I saw Marjory.

"Welcome, Pippa," said Marjory. "It's time for you to learn about the art of costumes. Come put your stuff in my office and see if you can find a chair."

Finding a chair—or anything else for that matter—wasn't easy, because every inch of Marjory's office, from the floor to the walls, was covered with things. The walls had color swatches, bits of fabric, lists, pictures of dogs, and postcards pinned to rows of bulletin boards.

"So can I start helping to make some of the costumes today?" I asked.

Marjory laughed and said, "Let's begin at the beginning so you understand what goes into the costumes."

Marjory explained that most ballets begin with the choreographer, who chooses or creates the ballet that will be performed. *Sleeping Beauty* is a "traditional" or "classical" ballet. That's the opposite of most modern ballets, which are often "abstract" because they use dance to explore an idea or image instead of telling a story with characters.

With *Sleeping Beauty*, the choreographer's role is to "stage" the performance. Instead of starting from nothing, the choreographer takes the original version, choreographed by Marius Petipa, and then adjusts it to reflect his or her idea of how the story should be told, sometimes changing the steps to suit the style and physique of the dancers.

"For example," Marjory said, "we are going to use choreography that was done by a very famous Russian dancer, Rudolf Nureyev. In the original choreography by Petipa, the male dancers had very little to do except lift the ballerinas. Prince Florimund was given only one short solo. But later, when Nureyev himself decided to dance the role of Prince Florimund in the version of *Sleeping Beauty* that he choreographed, he added two more male solos."

Choreographer and dancer Rudolf Nureyev performing in *The Sleeping Beauty* with the National Ballet of Canada in 1972

"That's something Verity would probably like to do, too," I said.

"Well, being the choreographer *and* the principal dancer is one way to make that happen," Marjory said, laughing. "But the choreographer has to have a vision of not only the steps that will be danced but also the setting where the dancing will happen."

"But hasn't all that been decided since *Sleeping Beauty* isn't a new ballet?" I asked.

"It depends," said Marjory. "The choreographer chooses a designer and then they work together to decide if, for instance, a Russian court of the 1600s would work better for the setting of the ballet instead of a French court or if it should take place in a completely different time period altogether."

"So then you start making the costumes?" I asked.

"Not quite," said Marjory. "But this *is* where the wardrobe department first gets involved. We go to meetings with the choreographer and the designer to understand what they are thinking. A designer like Santo Loquasto designs both the sets and the costumes, but there are also productions where those jobs are divided up, with separate costume and set designers. The important thing is that you don't want to have a jumble of ideas."

Marjory could see that I was still trying to understand how the whole designer thing worked.

"Since choreographers and costume and set designers have to work closely together, it's important that each person understand the style of the others. Many designers develop a signature style or way of working.

THE CHOREOGRAPHER

MUSIC

THE COSTUMES

"For example, Santo Loquasto is famous for his use of color and for layering his costumes with different materials. And Desmond Heeley, for instance, was a designer who was very special to me because he taught me so much of what I know. He was a beautiful painter and thought like an artist. Desmond was also a genius at using the most ordinary things, like masking tape, tin foil, and even air conditioner foam, to create parts of a costume or set design.

"But designers get inspiration from all kinds of places. It could be a museum painting or sculpture, the tile on a bathroom floor, what someone on the subway is wearing, or even the color of a vegetable."

Marjory stood up and pulled a large black binder labeled SLEEPING BEAUTY down from the shelf above her desk.

"We're almost there," she said. "Once we have the costume designer's sketches to work from, we have what are called 'production meetings.' That's when we make a lot of decisions, starting with the budget and the fabrics and whether we're going to build all new costumes, use old ones, or rework some existing ones. Once that's all done, everything is put together in what we call 'the bible.'

"Each ballet has its own set of bibles, and these are very, very, very important. Think of them as instruction books. Now let's look at *Sleeping Beauty*'s bible."

Marjory opened the bible for *Sleeping Beauty* and pointed out details as she flipped through it. "Choreography: Nureyev. Costumes: Nicholas Georgiadis. He designed the original costumes for Nureyev, and his design sketches are the ones we are using for this production.

"A bible is not only an archive; it has a practical purpose as well. This is how we keep track of all the costumes in a specific ballet. See how each page lists the character, the scene, and all the details we need to know about the costume? So we have swatches of fabric, the dimensions of the pattern, the types of decorations used on the costume, and the measurements of the dancer."

A ballet "bible" page, with fabrics, dimensions, and other costuming notes (left); a sketch of a costume, with details from the bible page, by Nicholas Georgiadis.

I was looking carefully at the page when Marjory said, "One more very important thing: Anyone can come in and use the *Sleeping Beauty* bible, but it never leaves this office.

"For today, I want you to study the bible, because it will give you a lot of important information, like how Nicholas Georgiadis based his designs on two historical periods."

"Louis XIV and Louis XV," I said, thankful that I had listened to Verity read *Behind Beauty*.

"Brilliant," said Marjory. "The hunting scene is when the period changes from Louis XIV's to Louis XV's. Pay close attention to the details so you can see how fashion changed after a hundred-year nap . . . which is what I will be doing after this season ends."

I was copying the page with the Lilac Fairy when Verity arrived to tell me that she was done with class for the day and that Mom was waiting in the lobby.

Verity looked over my shoulder, "That looks so good, Pippa."

I wrinkled my nose. "More like Georgiadis knockoff drawings."

"Huh?" said Verity, looking confused.

I explained who he was and then showed her how the bible was organized by characters.

"Marjory told me that in *Sleeping Beauty*, a lot of the characters come in groups, or *sets*, like the good fairies, the dancers in the court scenes, the huntsmen, and Carabosse's posse of bad fairies. Look—your costume is listed with children in the court scenes. And you *are* getting a new costume."

"Wow," said Verity. "That's so . . . so . . ."

"*Fabuleux*," I said.

"*Trés fabuleux*," said Verity.

MY TU-TU-TORIAL

The wardrobe department has a little kitchen with a table and chairs, and in the afternoons there are tea breaks. I was very excited this Wednesday to see a plate of cookies.

I was sitting with Ruth and Marjory, but a few minutes later Chris and Lily joined us.

"Is Pippa here?" I heard someone ask.

I looked around to see who had called my name and saw Cece come in.

"I found some articles about the wonderful Santo Loquasto for you," she said, handing me a folder.

"Thank you," I said, wondering if it would be rude to peek at them right away.

"Pull up a chair and have some tea," said Marjory to Cece. She looked around at her team. "Since we have so many experts here at the same time, this seems like the perfect moment to give Pippa a crash course on the tutu."

"We get so many questions about tutus that once a year the wardrobe department has an exhibit for the public to explain how they're made," Cece explained to me. "It's my duty as an archivist to supply books and pictures from the library for that exhibit. I'll go and grab a few of them now."

"I'll get an actual tutu," said Ruth.

"And I'll get my sketchbook," I said.

"Well then," said Marjory, "I'm going to get another cup of tea."

By the time Cece had returned, carrying a stack of books and folders, and Ruth had set up a tutu on a stand near the doorway, the kitchen was pretty crowded.

"Remember, I said 'a crash course,'" said Marjory, cyeing Cece's pile. "We have to get back to work."

"I'll just cover the high points," said Chris with a little grin.

"I'll give Pippa the long and short of it," Lily added.

"I won't skirt around the facts, though," said Ruth.

Everyone was laughing. Everyone, that is, but me. Clearly I needed some help with wardrobe humor.

Marjory noticed my confusion. "We're making some very bad puns about the tutu. I promise when Cece finishes her two-minute history, you will understand."

An example of an ankle-length tutu; print entitled
Medée, dans l'opéra de Jason et Medée, 1779

"Okay, here goes," said Cece. She explained that the "long" part of the story goes back to when ballet was part of court life and men performed the major dance parts. Women performed lesser roles and were expected to move with small, dainty steps that displayed elegance and modesty. Since they wore tight corsets and undergarments that practically cut off their breathing and long ankle-length, bell-shaped skirts, it's a wonder they could move at all.

By the 1800s, things had reversed; ballerinas had taken over the stage and men were now playing the smaller parts.

One of the most famous ballerinas, Marie Taglioni, made dance history in 1832 when she performed the title role in the ballet *The Sylph* at the Paris Opéra while wearing the first tutu. The style she wore is now called a "romantic" tutu. It was created for her by Eugène Lami, a French designer. Her tutu had a tight-fitted bodice, which revealed her neck and shoulders, and a bell-shaped skirt of white muslin and gauze that fell midway between her knees and ankles.

"This is the short part," I said.

"Bravo," said Marjory. "Now you can start making bad puns, too."

Lami's design recognized the new developments in ballet. His decision to shorten the skirt gave the audience a better view of Taglioni's footwork when she went *en pointe*—or danced on her toes in special ballet pointe shoes—for the first time in dance history. Pointe shoes, which are specially designed with stiff supports in the toe to help with balancing,

Marie Taglioni as La Sylphide; print entitled *La sylphide; souvenir d'adieu de Marie Taglioni,* 1845

hadn't been invented yet, so Taglioni did this in soft ballet slippers.

With its supernatural theme and dreamlike feeling, *The Sylph* was the first of what would come to be known as a "romantic" ballet.

"Things got a little less romantic, though," said Ruth.

Lami's tutu was widely copied for its beauty, but for a number of dancers it was a disaster. During the mid-nineteenth century, stages were lit with gaslights, and there were many stories of ballerina's skirts catching fire. In 1862, for example, twenty-one-year-old Emma Livery's skirt went up in flames during a rehearsal and led to her death.

"Yikes!" I said.

"But if you want to know what happens to the tutu, just remember that what goes down must go up," said Chris.

PANCAKES AND POWDERPUFFS

By "up," Chris meant the "classical" tutu, which is also called the pancake tutu because of its wide, deep, and very flat skirt. A classical tutu is made of twelve layers of tulle supported by

Tutus all stacked up

a wire hoop. Unlike the romantic tutu, which flows down, the pancake tutu sticks straight out. Its structure means that it sometimes continues to move on its own for a few beats after the dancer has finished moving. Although the classical tutu continues to be worn today, another tutu was invented in 1950 by one legendary woman.

"KARINSKA!" everyone shouted.

Barbara Karinska was born in Russia, where, as a child, she learned how to embroider, or sew delicate patterns into fabric with needle and thread. This became a skill she would use throughout her life. After leaving Russia and moving to

Paris with her daughter, she scraped together a living by crocheting wool flowers and making Russian headdresses decorated with pearls and ribbons, which she sold to costume designers and shopkeepers.

Word of Karinska's handiwork spread, but her career officially began when the director of a newly formed ballet company, the Ballets Russe de Monte Carlo, asked Karinska to make all the costumes for their first season. Desperate for work, she accepted the job despite never having made a tutu.

The designer for the ballet company was an artist named Christian Bérard, and the choreographer was George Balanchine, who would become Karinska's most famous collaborator.

It was up to Karinska to calculate how much fabric was needed and how to cut, fit, and decorate all the costumes based on Bérard's designs. Through a great deal of trial and error, which involved ripping out stitches and re-cutting fabric, Karinska not only taught herself how to make a tutu but constructed a bodice that was lighter, more flexible, and fit better than anything that had been made before.

In 1933 Balanchine moved to the United States, and six years later Karinska joined him at the New York City Ballet.

Over the years, she created thousands of costumes for the company. Balanchine's choreography style, which required dancers to move quickly and close together, did not work well with the pancake tutus, which collided during performances because of their wire hoops. Karinska resolved this problem by creating what is known as the powder-puff tutu, which is a feat of engineering as well as one of beauty. Her designs are admired for having the fullness of a pancake tutu without the annoyance of a wire hoop.

Karinska also famously layered different colors of fabric together, as she believed one solid color looked dead under the stage lights. And her tutus' exquisite craftsmanship wasn't just on the outside; the undersides were hand-sewn with the same care and included details like tiny embroidered flowers that couldn't be seen by the audience but made the dancer feel special.

Her costumes are still at the New York City Ballet along with some of the original decorations and fabrics she used.

But that wasn't the end of my tu-tu-torial.

"Now you have to see the actual parts and how they're put together," said Marjory.

Each part of the tutu, whether a pancake tutu or a powder-puff tutu, is made separately and then assembled.

The top part of the costume is called the *bodice*. The bodice is like a tank top and includes the neckline and armholes, and it ends at the waist. A technique called *boning* is used, where stiff material is added to help the bodice hold its shape. A long time ago whalebones were used, which explains the name. Now wide steel bones or plastic bones are used.

The *basque* is the part of the garment that covers the dancer from the waist to the hip, connecting the skirt to the bodice.

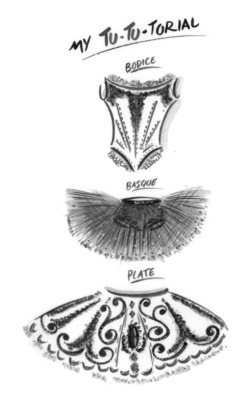

MY TU-TU-TORIAL

BODICE

BASQUE

PLATE

The *skirt* begins with a panty (like a granny panty) so you have something to attach the skirt layers to. There are twelve to sixteen layers in total. The softest netting goes closest to the leg. Each layer is wider than the one below. Depending on the style, a wire hoop can be put into the center layer of the skirt to help the tutu stand out straight.

The *plate* is the final piece of fabric, and it goes on top of the skirt layers. It is decorated with sequins, beads, or faux jewels. *Faux* (the *x* is silent, I learned today) is a nicer, French way of saying *fake*.

DID YOU KNOW?

- It takes one hundred and twenty hours to make a basic tutu and even longer if there are decorations.
- It can cost several thousand dollars to make one tutu.
- Tutus are hung upside down to help keep their shape.

"You know, Pippa," said Cece, "one of the things I learned from my research is that ballet and fashion have a long history of inspiring each other that still continues today."

"Maybe I'll be able to do both," I said.

"Well then," said Ruth, winking at Marjory, "we'll have to conclude this tutu review with one last thing. You have to take the tutu off that mannequin."

It turns out that removing a tutu from a stand is not as easy as it sounds. The stand is tippy, and pretty soon I felt like I was one half of a wrestling match. In this corner we have Pippa, fumbling with layers and layers of netting, and in the other we have a tutu that will not give up the stand!

When the stand finally tipped over and I was on the ground, Ruth stretched out a hand to help me up.

"Now you've been initiated into the wardrobe department," Marjory said, laughing. "No one can get a tutu off its stand when they first start, but you'll learn."

Ding-ding! With a little coaching from Ruth and Marjory, I was back in the ring, and on my fourth try, I got that tutu off the stand and held it up in the air.

GARGOYLES AND ROSETTES

Between ballet class and rehearsals, Verity, Enid, and Noelle become inseparable and even started calling themselves "the three supers." So it was only natural that the next time Verity came to pick me up from the wardrobe department, Noelle and Enid were trailing behind her.

"I hope it's okay that we came with Verity," said Noelle nervously when she saw Marjory.

"Of course," replied Marjory. "You're cast members, after all. While you're here, would you like to take a peek at some of the costumes the Lilac Fairy and Carabosse will wear?"

Lilac Fairy costume from Nureyev's
production of *The Sleeping Beauty*

"Yes, please," the three supers all said at once. They practically swooned when Marjory held up the gown the Lilac Fairy wears in the Prologue.

"That is the most *beeyootiful* costume I have ever seen," said Noelle.

"It is lovely," agreed Marjory. "The costumes for the Lilac Fairy and Carabosse show the theme of the ballet, which is the fight between good and evil."

"I never thought about that," said Noelle.

Princess Aurora might be the heroine of *Sleeping Beauty*, but the Lilac Fairy is the good fairy stuck with all the cleanup. She has to undo part of the curse, put the entire kingdom to sleep for a century, get Prince Florimund to quit brooding and find Aurora, and, as if that's not enough, deliver the blessing at the wedding.

Carabosse costume from Nureyev's
production of *The Sleeping Beauty*

Next, Marjory showed us one of Carabosse's costumes.

"When the Lilac Fairy and Carabosse face off in the prologue, you need to see two strong, confident characters who are each determined to win the battle," she said. "In many productions, Carabosse wears all black to play up her image as a wicked witch or old crone—just the type we expect would be horrible enough to plant a curse on a baby.

"This costume is designed to show how Carabosse sees herself—as someone important who's angry that she wasn't invited to baby Aurora's party. She may not be beautiful in the traditional fairy-tale style, but she's powerful and doesn't mind interrupting the party to leave Aurora's mom and dad with something to really worry about."

Moral of the story: When you're told to invite everyone in the kingdom, it means invite *everyone.*

Unfortunately for Carabosse, Marjory tells us that by the second act she's a train wreck. She's hunched over and looks defeated and smaller. Her wig and makeup are a mess, and she needs a makeover. Her power is gone, her nails are an embarrassment, and a comeback is unlikely. Mean girls, take note.

Not so for the Lilac Fairy. Three acts and a hundred years haven't aged her a bit. She looks charming and graceful, which shows what happens when you have a good heart.

On the other hand, to be fair to Carabosse, no one really likes being ignored.

That Saturday there was going to be a rehearsal, and Verity had gone all out planning the first Super Saturday Sleepover for the three supers.

"Did you order the special cupcakes?" she asked Mom for the millionth time.

"Yes," said Mom for the millionth time.

"I think you're being a little ridiculous," I said. "Nothing is going to ruin your sleepover." Famous last words, especially coming from the person who ended up ruining all of Verity's carefully laid plans.

I didn't realize that all it took was one trip to the wardrobe department to make me a celebrity with two of the three supers.

That Saturday, I was sitting on the couch squeezed between Ballet Thing One and Ballet Thing Two (while Ballet Thing Three stood nearby looking annoyed), when they started asking me a million questions. It turned out that they also provided the answers.

"Have you seen some of the other costumes? Duh—of course you have," said Noelle.

"I can't believe you work there. You are so lucky," said Enid.

"She doesn't actually work there," said Verity. "She's more like an apprentice."

The real trouble began when Noelle held up the remote and suggested we watch *Off the Rack*.

"I thought we were going to watch *Tears on My Slippers*," said Verity. "It's this really sad movie about a ballet dancer who—"

"This will be more fun," said Enid, "especially with our fashion-and-costume expert."

Verity didn't look thrilled about the change in plans. "I'll go get some snacks," she offered. "Does anyone want me to make smoothies?"

"Shhh, it's starting," said Enid, pointing to Baskette's unsmiling face on the screen.

"Dezzzigners, what makes a hat a hat? What makes a purse a purse? Is it what they are made of or how they are made? These are the universal questions we ask ourselves."

"I have never asked that question," said Noelle. "Ever."

"I don't even understand the question," said Enid.

"Your designment will challenge you to cross boundaries and question everything you know. It will require ingenuity and creativity."

"I am so confused," said Enid. "What are they doing?"

It turned out that the only boundary the designers had to cross was a busy city street. After that they each needed their ingenuity and creativity to find materials from a hardware store, a pet-supply store, or a post office to make an accessory.

Verity returned with the tray of famous, specially ordered cupcakes, complete with the three supers' names written in curlicue icing. Noelle was so caught up with the drama on *Off the Rack* that she picked up a cupcake without looking at it.

"Oops—I just ate yours, Enid," she said, giggling.

"Then I'll eat yours," said Enid, holding up one of the *Noelle* cupcakes. "Mmm."

"These are delicious, Verity," said Noelle, whose mouth was covered with frosting.

For one brief second, Verity perked up.

"Coming up next: The designers face the judges in the lineup."

"Whoa whoa whoa," said Pinky Vogue, shielding her eyes from a neon-green-yellow-and-pink duct-tape clutch. "Please do not tell me the store ran out of black duct tape, not to mention gaffer tape and electrical tape."

"I thought that would be too obvious," whimpered the designer.

"I think neon is a little too obvious," said Pinky Vogue and then broke out the signature phrase she uses on her blog: "Am I right, ladies?"

"She's so mean," said Verity.

"It's part of the show," said Enid.

"I'm not so sure," said Noelle. "I think she might actually be mean."

"No one in the wardrobe department is mean—that's for sure," I said.

"You have to tell us more later," said Enid.

Austin Tornado loved the hat woven from the mesh strips used for lawn chairs.

"The hose totally kicks it up a notch," he said.

"The spigot is what speaks to me," said Baskette.

"I wonder what it's telling her," I said.

"Verity, your sister is so funny," said Noelle.

"Hilarious," muttered Verity.

The best part of the show is when the judges fight.

"I respect the fact that you have no idea if what you've made is a hat or a bag or both," said Baskette, holding something that didn't look like either.

"I do not respect the fact that you don't have a clue what it is," said Leticia Blum in her famously stern voice. "I think it's completely feeble."

When Austin Tornado objected to a belt glued together from flea-and-tick collars, Pinky Vogue stood up on her chair and said, "Mr. Tornado, you shouldn't even be in fashion."

"Really?" sneered Austin Tornado. "Why don't I make a pair of sneakers out of chew toys for you?"

"That could be kind of retro," said Baskette as Leticia Blum lowered her head onto the table.

The garment bag ended up going to the designer who insisted that he didn't need to change a leaf-collection bag since it was already a bag.

"That was such a great episode," said Noelle. "Pippa, you should be on *Off the Rack*."

"You could make one of your own designs and send it in," said Enid.

"I think you have to be able to sew," Verity commented.

"Not after what we saw tonight," said Enid. "She could just staple something together."

It was fun being the center of attention, and it's possible that I got a little carried away when I brought out a book Marjory had lent me about costumes and made it sound like I was doing research. I may have even hinted that I could possibly show them some of the tutus "we were building."

Mom appeared in her robe and slippers to say good night. "What happened to the *Sleeping Beauty* Super Spa?" she asked, referring to the potions and lotions Verity had set up in the bathroom.

"The same thing that's been happening all night," said Verity, glowering at me.

"Pippa, maybe it's time for you to go to bed, too," suggested Mom. "Give the supers a little time on their own."

"It's fine," said Noelle. "We're having fun."

"Pippa can be our new SUPERSTAR," said Enid.

I'm pretty sure that was the moment Verity decided she had the unfairest sister in all the land.

A BOLT OF BALLROOM BLUE WITH A HINT OF AZURE AND A TOUCH OF CERULEAN

The sleepover brouhaha really blew up on Sunday. Mom sat us down in the living room and then waffled back and forth, trying to make us see both sides.

"Your friends are excited about the wardrobe department," Mom told Verity. "You can't blame Pippa for that."

"You were the one who brought them there," I pointed out. "I can't help it if everyone was more interested in costumes and watching *Off the Rack* than in a drippy movie about some ballerina."

Bad move. Mom switched over to me and said, "But, Pippa, you knew how hard Verity worked to plan everything, and you should have excused yourself after watching *Off the Rack.*"

I might have agreed and possibly even apologized, but just then Verity shot me one of her smarmy looks, so instead I said, "It is not my fault I am a person of interest."

"Isn't a person of interest usually someone suspected of committing a crime?" asked Dad as he walked through the room.

"Well, that part is true," said Verity, storming out and making sure she had the last word.

When I say the last word, I mean it. Verity continued to avoid saying anything to me for the rest of Sunday, Monday, and Tuesday. When Mom dropped us off at ballet on Wednesday, Verity told her, "I'm not going to pick you-know-who up after class today," before stomping off. It was a very dramatic exit, but unfortunately she also left her ballet bag in the car.

"I don't suppose you would consider . . . ?" Mom began.

There was no way I was going to deliver anything to Miss High-and-Haughty. Mom gave a long sigh and came inside with me.

"Pippa, pressing the button over and over will not make

it come any faster," said Mom as we waited for the elevator. "Nor will tapping your feet."

A second later, the elevator arrived and the doors opened.

As we got in, I said to Mom, "I think the tapping feet really did speed things up."

Mom went to Verity's classroom, and I went to the wardrobe department.

"You're going to work with Chris in the Fabric and Notion Room today," Marjory told me. "Once the sketches are finalized, the next step is choosing, or what we call *sourcing*, the fabrics, which can mean going to a local fabric store or scouring the globe to find the exact tulle silk or particular texture and color of fabric you need."

The fabric room looked like a giant cave. Industrial shelves held long cylinders wrapped in every possible color and texture of material, all stacked on top of one another. We found Chris on a ladder, tugging on a roll of something that was pale pink and squeezed between two other rolls, which were slightly different shades of pink.

"I'll make sure Pippa has a lot of good material when she leaves here," said Chris as Marjory waved goodbye. "Actually, you need to know an encyclopedia's worth of information about textiles. There's a science to fabrics, depending on whether they're made from natural fibers or not and how they react to different conditions, like if we want to paint designs on them or use strong lighting against them onstage.

"Most dance costumes use silks, satins, tulle, and cotton, but sometimes they use other materials, too. You'll see how some of the costumes are layered with different fabrics. One reason we do this is to cut down on costs by mixing inexpensive materials with silks and lace, which can be very pricey."

Pippa's Mini Textile Encyclopedia (not in alphabetical order):

Icky: Perspiration can ruin fragile fabrics, like silk or satin, and can shorten the life of a costume. (Not to mention how gross sweat stains look.) So behind every beautiful bodice is a layer of sturdy cotton backing, which is there to absorb sweat.

Net rash: Tutus are tough on male dancers. They get net rash on their faces and necks, which rub against the tutu fabric when they lift ballerinas.

Technology: not just for devices but also for inventing new materials. Ballet tights used to be made from elasticized cotton. Thank you, Lycra and spandex, for putting an end to all that bagging and sagging.

Thread (No Spooling Around!): Who knew there were so many different kinds of thread? Cotton, polyester, metallic (for embroidery and decoration), silk, and glow-in-the-dark melting nylon, which melts in heat above 250 degrees Fahrenheit and holds fabric together.

Thread colors: They have names like nail polish—Mohave Mauve, Petunia Pink, and Toucan Orange. (I guess that's more exciting than a name like #001.)

Wolf wear: *Sleeping Beauty* has a wolf, cat, bird, and, in some productions, rats. These costumes use a combination of fabrics—plastic, fur, felt, metal cording, gauze, and cotton.

Bolt: Each long roll of fabric is called a *bolt*. Bolts are either forty or a hundred yards long. (See: Humiliating Incident.)

Humiliating Incident: knocking over bolts of different sizes and watching them unroll all over the floor.

After Chris and I finished rerolling and stacking the bolts, he said, "Well, that's a wrap for this Wednesday."

I went to say goodbye to Marjory, and she invited me to come by the wardrobe department on Saturday to see how dye, paint, and other techniques can change the way fabric looks.

"Consider it *Fabrics: the Sequel*," she said.

That was a pretty great surprise to end the day, but it wasn't the last one.

"Come on, let's go," said Verity, who was waiting for me at the door. Then she added, "Enid is hosting the second Super Saturday Sleepover this weekend at her house."

"That will be fun," I said. "You know, three is really the perfect number for a sleepover."

And for the rest of the week, we lived happily ever after.

BONUS SATURDAY

"Back here," came a voice.

Mom and I found Marjory in the Dyeing, Washing, Drying, and Pressing Room, wearing a long white apron and huge rubber gloves that went up past her elbows.

"Don't tell me you do laundry, too!" Mom exclaimed, eyeing the washing machine and dryer as if she had never seen appliances like them before.

"Believe it or not, in the costume world, these are a sign of modern times," said Marjory. "In the early 1900s ballet companies didn't have laundry facilities, so the costumes were incredibly stinky. Now we can have costumes specially cleaned, but we also have a lot of leotards and tights to wash, and sometimes shirts like this one . . ."

Mom opened her mouth and gasped.

"You've seen a man's white shirt before," I said.

"Well, maybe not one that belongs to a famous soloist," said Marjory, pointing to the name on the hanger.

"Would you like to stay?" Marjory asked Mom. Of course, Mom was only too happy to trade an afternoon of boring errands for a chance to put on an apron and join us.

"A designer will indicate colors, textures, or patterns and even suggest certain fabrics to us," said Marjory. "But sometimes a fabric alone isn't enough to give a costume the look it needs. That's when textile painters and dyers roll up their sleeves and get into the illusion business."

I had a feeling my textile encyclopedia was no longer going to be mini.

"Dye is also used to freshen up costumes when a color starts to fade," said Marjory, "or to create a particular color, like the one for the Bluebird character in *Sleeping Beauty*'s wedding scene. Now, without further ado, let the demonstration begin."

First you put on huge rubber gloves.

The dye goes in a large vat with very, very hot water and sometimes salt or vinegar. It's called a dye bath. (Do not get in.)

Once you've put the fabric into the vat, you have to shake and stir it using a long spoon to get the color absorbed into the fabric. Marjory says the technical term is to *agitate* the fabric. This term can also be used with siblings and parents but not in the same way. When the fabric gets wet, it feels really heavy and gets harder to stir around.

Next you need a device called an *extractor*, which squeezes the water out of the fabric. Then the fabric is hung up to dry on a clothesline. If the color isn't right, then the whole process gets repeated.

Colors in ballet costumes are very important, because they tell you about the character and also make some of the principal dancers stand out from the company dancers. In *Sleeping Beauty*, Princess Aurora's costumes are a different color in each act to show how she changes from a young sixteen-year-old to a fully grown woman on her wedding day.

Princess Aurora's costume in act 1 from Nureyev's production of *The Sleeping Beauty*

In act 2, Princess Aurora is a young woman who falls in love with Prince Florimund after he wakes her up from the world's longest nap. (I think she even sleeps in a tutu.) One of the perks of being a princess is that no one else can wear the color or style of her dress.

Princess Aurora's costume in act 3 of
Nureyev's production of
The Sleeping Beauty

Act 3 is the grand finale, with the wedding of Princess Aurora and Prince Florimund. (No wonder she needs so much sleep—it's party, party, party for this princess.) Her wedding costume is a white-and-gold tutu to show that she is now grown up as well as to symbolize that goodness triumphed over Carabosse's nasty shenanigans.

Needless to say, Carabosse doesn't make the guest list for the wedding, but by then she really doesn't have anything suitable to wear, anyway. Here are the storybook characters who make the cut: Little Red Riding Hood and the Gray Wolf, Cinderella, Tom Thumb, the Bluebird, the White Cat, and Puss in Boots.

There's always one guest who is the life of the party, and at this wedding it's the Bluebird.

The Bluebird's costume from
Nureyev's production of
The Sleeping Beauty

He dances with Princess Aurora in a *pas de deux* (pronounced *pah deh doo*), or duct, and takes over the dance floor with a spectacular solo. He jumps across the stage, doing a move called *brisé volé* (pronounced *bree-zay vo-lay*), which means something along the lines of "beating your feet like a bird."

Not any old blue will do for his tights and costume, so a combination of bold, vivid shades are combined and then the costume is decorated with feathers.

More Notes for Pippa's Mini Textile Encyclopedia (still not in alphabetical order):

Hand: Who knew fabrics had hands? In textiles, the word *hand* is used to describe the feel or texture of the fabric. Dye can change the color of a fabric without affecting the way it feels. If the feel *does* change, designers would say they're "changing the hand."

Breaking down the fabric: describes a process to make a costume look old, worn, distressed, faded, or damaged.

Tricks of the trade: A cheese grater can give fabric small rips and tears. Bleaching, burning, and tearing are some of the other ways to transform or artificially age costumes.

Textile paint: feels more like glue than regular paint.

Painting: can also mean using sponges, blocks, stencils, or silk screens in addition to regular painting.

Gunking: a way to give inexpensive fabrics a different surface texture and look by adding sequins, glitter, powder, stones, dirt, etc.

Ombre: a technique where multiple shades of a color fade into one another. Similar to a paint swatch, where you see a dark color followed by a lighter shade of the same color.

Double ombre: has different colors on either end, and the place in the middle where the colors overlap create a different color altogether. For example, yellow on one end and blue on the other gives you green in the middle.

I felt like a whole new world had opened up for me. A world of dyeing and painting and gunking.

"Did you know there's a brand-new art store that just opened on the next block?" I mentioned casually to Mom in the car. "I bet they have dye."

"I think I know where this is going," said Mom.

"Ms. Von der Bleek always says to follow your inspiration."

"Well, just make sure you follow it down to the basement if your inspiration is messy," said Mom.

WHOPPERS, POPPERS, AND JUDYS

Mom had suggested I keep a low profile around the supers for a little while, but when we arrived at ballet today we ran right into Enid, who yelled "SUPERSTAR!" as soon as she saw me in the lobby saying hello to Ida.

"I bet you'll be doing something more exciting than practicing *pliés*," she said before Verity pulled her away.

Sometimes it is very hard to be me.

But when I walked into the wardrobe department, I decided that it's also pretty nice to be me.

The door to Marjory's office was open, but I still knocked. "Reporting for duty," I announced.

Marjory patted the chair where I usually sat. "Are you ready to visit the construction zone?" she said.

"Is this where the building-the-costume part happens?" I asked.

"Yes," said Marjory. "Today you're going to work with our resident cutting and draping team, Ruth and Chris. Remember, they're responsible for making the patterns that we use to turn a sketch into a three-dimensional costume."

"Those must be really hard jobs," I said.

"Believe it or not, the techniques for making patterns haven't changed that much since the sixteenth century. It used to be that if you wanted to be a cutter, you had to train as an apprentice for seven years. At the beginning you were only allowed to hand the cutter their tools and tidy up, and eventually you were allowed to sew pockets."

"Seven years?" I yelped.

Marjory stood up and motioned toward the door. "We'd better not lose another minute."

"This will be good training for Pippa if she ever works as a *petite mains* in haute couture," Marjory said to Ruth and Chris, who were sitting at long tables across from each other.

I didn't know what *petite mains* meant, but I *did* know a little something about haute couture. First, I knew it's pronounced *oat koo-tur*. Second, it means "high dressmaking" in French, or high-fashion clothing that is created by a designer and made by hand from start to finish. I've devoted a lot of time to picturing myself as the superfamous designer who comes onto the runway at the end of my supersuccessful fashion show in New York or Paris, wearing gigantic sunglasses.

I hadn't gotten around to thinking about the making-the-clothes-by-hand part.

And after just a few minutes with Ruth, Chris, and Marjory, I learned that haute couture workrooms are called ateliers (pronounced *a-tel-yays*). They also told me that ateliers are where people who do all the cutting, draping, and stitching work, and those people are called *petite mains*, or "little hands."

The techniques used to make costumes in the wardrobe department were the same ones you needed to work in an haute couture atelier. As far as my own *petite mains* were concerned, they had no idea how to do anything either in French or in English.

"Cutting and draping are the two ways to figure out the pattern we need to use in order to stitch and assemble the garment," Ruth explained.

"In an atelier, the tailoring, or *cutting*, and the dressmaking, or *draping*, are done in different rooms," added Chris.

"*Tailoring* refers to making suits, jackets, and trousers, whether for a man or for a woman. We also call it cutting because of how we work with the fabrics, which are stiffer and heavier," said Chris.

"Draping uses soft and flowy fabrics that we work with on a dress form," said Ruth. "A word you'll hear a lot is *silhouette* (pronounced *sil-oo-et*), which means the general shape or outline of a body. It's like costume geometry."

I was beginning to understand why it took seven years before someone could use a pair of scissors.

Ruth went on, "Depending on what you do with fabric, it can become any number of different shapes: triangular, boxy, puffy, fitted . . . Those shapes can actually change the way someone's body appears by emphasizing certain parts, like the waist or the shoulders. In a costume, the silhouette tells you a lot about the character a dancer is portraying."

"The plan is for you to work with Chris and learn about

cutting and then switch to draping with Ruth, after which you will be drooping from everything you've learned," said Marjory, who had to leave for a meeting.

Chris pulled over a stool for me and held up a pretty ratty-looking jacket. "As you can see, Prince Florimund is in dire need of some new hunting duds. In this case, we can use this old costume as an example to copy when we make a new one. But we're going to pretend that we've never made this jacket before so that you can understand the whole process.

"We have the designer's sketch to give us the vision of how the costume should look," he said, pointing to a copy of it taped on the table. "For a period costume, we also do some historical research on what an eighteenth-century fancy-pants like Prince Florimund would wear."

Members of the French aristocracy, like Prince Florimund, would have worn a suit called <u>habit à la française</u> (pronounced <u>abee a la fron ses</u>) to show their importance. The suit had three different pieces:
- The outer coat or justaucorps (pronounced <u>joost-uh-cors</u>)

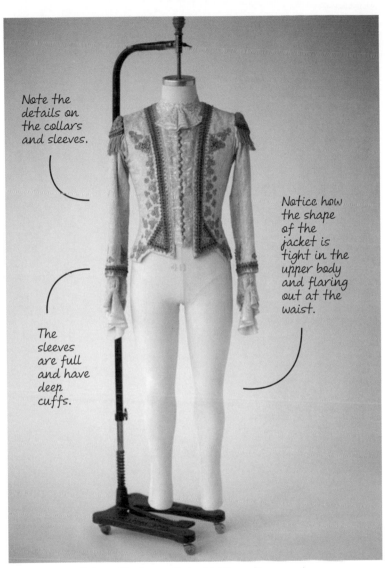

Note the details on the collars and sleeves.

Notice how the shape of the jacket is tight in the upper body and flaring out at the waist.

The sleeves are full and have deep cuffs.

Prince Florimund's jacket from Nureyev's production of *The Sleeping Beauty*

- Inner waistcoat, which looks like a vest
- Breeches/pants that extend from the waist to the knees
- The justaucorps was lengthened to the knee, and the tail in the back was split to make it possible to ride horses.

CUTTING

DRAPING

"Our job is not to do a perfect historical reproduction but to give the audience an impression of the character and time period through the silhouette," explained Chris. "And at the same time, we must construct a costume that allows the dancer to move."

FLAT PATTERN-MAKING

Draw a pattern for each part of the jacket onto kraft or tissue paper.

Each pattern piece is then traced onto the fabric.

A mock-up, or _toile_, using muslin is made before the final pattern pieces are used on the real fabric.

"You have to understand the different ways to cut fabric. It depends on whether you are trying to construct a sleeve or the front of a jacket, for example," said Chris, showing me some samples he had done.

Then he handed me some pattern pieces and muslin and told me to practice tracing and cutting.

"Not to get all boast-y, but I have been using scissors since kindergarten."

A little while later, I wasn't feeling quite so boast-y. My muslin cutout pieces were crooked and messy and looked nothing like the pattern pieces.

"These look like a squirrel got ahold of some scissors," I complained to Chris.

"Not too shabby for a squirrel," said Chris. "You both just need to keep practicing. But I still have one more thing to show you before you begin your long walk to the other table with Ruth."

Prince Florimund is keeping a secret under that jacket.

Here are a few tricks of the trade I learned. What looks like a whole jacket is actually two pieces: a vest and a separate shirt.

With period costumes, the armhole is cut higher up so the dancer can raise their arms. Elastic is added to give the side seams some stretch and make it easier to move.

Cutter's Tools

THIMBLE

NOTCHER

BODKIN

CLOSURES

WHOPPERS

POPPERS

SEAM RIPPER

TRACING WHEEL

"I'll be right back with a Judy," said Ruth.

I was expecting to see her return with a person, but instead Judy turned out to be a headless mannequin.

"Draping is a way to sculpt fabric into the shape you want," said Ruth, hanging a long flowing piece of silk on the Judy. "With draping, just like with cutting or tailoring, you begin with the sketch. This helps you understand the silhouette you are trying to create. You have to experiment with tucking and folding the fabric in different ways to get the shape that you want.

"Later we'll make a pattern as well, but first we experiment with the fabric by hanging it on the Judy to see how it falls and folds."

Ruth gave me some silk, chiffon, and a kind of smooth jersey so I could compare how it felt to work with different weights of fabric.

"Imagine that you're hanging a curtain," she advised. "Pull it back with a tie, let it hang straight, or try folding it to one side."

As I was pinning and folding, I imagined myself on *Off the Rack*. I could hear Austin Tornado saying, "I love the dramatic silhouette you've created with your gown, Pippa."

"It's so original and new, yet classic and old," Baskette would add.

"Shut the door," said Pinky Vogue.

"Pippa, it's time to go."

"Pippa!"

I looked up, and instead of Pinky Vogue, I saw Verity looking confused and impatient.

Ruth's Judy was wrapped in a flowing fabric that she had sculpted into a blouse-y top. It had beautiful folds that were neatly pinned. You could almost wear it the way it was.

My Judy looked like someone had dumped a pile of sheets on her. There were pins sticking out dangerously in all sorts of places.

"Mom's waiting," she said.

"This is a Judy," I said.

"Who?" said Verity.

I turned the mannequin to face her.

"Good thing she doesn't have a head, so she can't see what a mess I made of her dress," I said.

I can't be sure, but I think Verity may have smiled.

THE RULES OF THE JEWELS

It was a week later, and I couldn't believe how much there still was left to learn. When I entered the costume shop, Marjory held Lily and Lisa's hands in the air and proclaimed, "Meet the stitchers—the unsung heroes of any wardrobe department. To do this job, you need the skills of a surgeon and a laser eye for details."

Here's another thing you need to be able to do: SEW.

- even basting stitch
- uneven basting stitch
- running stitch
- backstitch
- slip stitch
- drawing stitch
- fell stitch
- chain stitch
- buttonhole stitch
- whipstitch
- cross your hand stitch (or zigzag stitch)

"I leave Pippa in your capable hands," said Marjory, blowing a kiss in our direction. "Back to the computer for me."

"My hands aren't all that capable," I warned, in case either Lily or Lisa wanted me to start whipstitching something right away.

"Not to worry," said Lisa. "You can always take sewing lessons. If you end up in a wardrobe department, your stitching needs to be done carefully and very neatly. A costume not only needs to look beautiful but be strong enough to handle all the twists and turns that dancers perform onstage."

"But we do have a plan for you we think you'll like," said Lily, turning me around to face a cabinet that looked like the old-fashioned card catalogues you see in libraries.

"Now check out the drawers," Lily instructed.

I opened one and then another and then another. There were fabric flowers, sequins, beads, feathers, and buttons of every possible size, color, and material. There were semi-precious stones that looked like they had been plucked from a pirate chest and small pieces of fabric decorated with intricately embroidered patterns, tassels, braids, and trims.

In short—bling city.

"If a costume needs any kind of decoration, this is where you'll find it," said Lily. "Or not."

"But don't think you won't be learning anything," said Lisa.

"Have a seat and prepare for the greatest SHOW-AND-TELL EVER!" they said together.

Lisa explained that every button, braid, and bead is selected at the same time as the fabric. This is so the designer can see how the decorations and fabric will look together. Then the stitchers must figure out the best technique to sew or attach the embellishments *very securely* to the costume.

"Even something this small is dangerous if it falls off

when a dancer is performing," said Lily, holding up a tiny blue bead.

"I guess it's sequins and not pride that comes before a fall," I said.

Which brings us to . . .

Lisa and Lily taught me that the technique of adding decorations to costumes is called *appliqué* (pronounced *app-lee-kay*, but with a French feeling). It was first used by the ancient Egyptians. (This is the kind of information that makes you feel supersmart.) You use special thread to either create a design or

Various jewels and gems, as seen up close

pattern or to sew decorations onto the costume directly or on a piece of muslin fabric that will be attached to the costume.

The whole afternoon felt like a party, especially after Lisa and Lily gave me a huge swag bag filled with baubles. When I got home, I went straight to my atelier, emptied everything out on my bed, and made up a little game.

PIPPA'S RULES OF THE JEWELS GAME

- pick a character
- pick a swatch of fabric for that character
- decorate
- add shiny things
- might even learn to sew

SWAP DAY

At school yesterday, Mr. Greenberg caught me secretly drawing instead of working on a math sheet.

"I'm guessing decimals are not as important to you as costume designs," he said.

"The thing is," I explained, "when *Sleeping Beauty* opens, I won't be going to the wardrobe department anymore. How will I remember everything if I don't put it in my sketchbook?"

"I understand," Mr. Greenberg said, "but I am concerned about how you will remember what to do with these decimals for the next quiz."

I didn't want to say that next year, when Verity was back in ballet class and I was stuck waiting in the hall, I would have plenty of time to work on decimals.

The supers had started going to rehearsals on Saturdays, and tonight's sleepover was at our house. To avoid a repeat of last time, Dad and I headed out to a movie.

When we came home we found the supers sprawled in front of the TV, dressed like three hot-air balloons. Their legs were covered with thick, speckled, woolen legwarmers that looked like hairballs a bunch of cats had coughed up.

I didn't know what to say, but it didn't matter, because the supers all started talking at once.

"Swap day—"

"Dancers donate stuff from lockers—"

"Real dance shorts—"

Translation: Every few months, all the unclaimed dance clothes from the lost-and-found and anything the company dancers want to swap get put out on a big table for people to take.

"We figured we should try to look more professional since we're supers," added Enid.

"I wonder why no one else wanted any of this stuff," said Verity, rubbing her leg.

Good Part: Everyone including Verity wanted to play Pippa's Rules of the Jewels Game.

Bad Part: It didn't take long to find out why their legwarmers had been discarded.

I was in my room when I heard screeching and yipping coming out of Verity's room.

The three supers had been scratching and itching and discovered little red bumps where the legwarmers had covered their bare skin.

Mom's diagnosis: mite bites.

Cure: calamine lotion for the legs, and a garbage bag for the legwarmers.

Moral of the story: Sometimes things aren't claimed for a reason.

Also: Verity might not be destined to have the perfect sleepover, but at least this time no one could blame me.

A TROLLEY RIDE AND
A SURPRISE

"Things are in a little bit of a tizzy," said Marjory when I arrived at her office.

One of the dancers was injured, and Ruth needed to fit the dancer taking her place with a tutu.

Another ballet company was renting costumes for a production of *Giselle* and a group of people were packing up trunks in the storage room.

Chris was trying to track down a missing fabric order.

Before Marjory could tell me what I was going to do, her

phone rang. I got up to leave so she could have some privacy, but she motioned for me to stay put.

"What!" Marjory said. "You mean right now—this minute—at the theater?"

She hung up the phone and looked over at me. "There's someone I'd like you to meet at the theater. Let's go."

On the trolley ride over, Marjory told me about how the theater had been rebuilt and expanded and was now very modern and a much nicer space for seeing the performances.

This was interesting, but not nearly as interesting as the phone call in her office.

I felt a little important walking in through the back entrance, where the security guard waved us through. The only people around were part of the ballet. A dancer stood alone in the middle of the stage while a spotlight shone over her.

"Hello," said a man coming up the aisle. I didn't know who he was, but there was something familiar about him.

"Pippa, this is someone I thought you'd like to meet," said Marjory. "The one and only Santo Loquasto."

I opened my mouth and tried to speak but ended up sputtering out a string of words that didn't actually make a sentence.

"I . . . You . . . Most beautiful sketch . . . Love . . . Want to be . . ."

"Santo and I have been trying to meet for months," explained Marjory. "We want him to design the sets and costumes for a ballet that's scheduled two years from now."

"At the last minute I had to come to your city on other business," said Santo, "and so here I am."

"And how lucky you chose a Wednesday, so Pippa could meet you," said Marjory.

Santo said, "My favorite part of this whole process is the beginning, when you have to figure out how you're going to do it."

"How do you come up with your ideas?" I asked.

"When I work with a ballet choreographer, the music is often the starting point for the overall concept in terms of how the ballet will look and feel. Some ideas start with a color or a shape, and designers find inspiration everywhere: museums, movies, someone's outfit . . . I've even gotten an idea from looking at a garbage bag."

"Amazing," I said. "How did that idea work?"

"Well," said Santo, "we had a scene with a big storm, and I wanted the costumes to play up the idea of flaming water. Ideally, we would have used the garbage bags as costumes, but instead we used blue and white leotards."

I nodded, remembering the tutu fiascos with gaslights.

"Those were pretty incredible sets," said Marjory. "We had a painted backcloth of a ship lying on its side that was built to break apart. Santo is part magician and part engineer and a genius at details."

"Not me," I said. "I failed a test on mixed fractions because I didn't pay attention to the numbers on the bottom."

"Well, I grew up in Wilkes-Barre, Pennsylvania, where I was kicked out of kindergarten," said Santo. "Luckily for me, my mother found a children's theater class instead."

"Luckily for me, I lost my sketchbook and Marjory found it," I said.

"I would like to see this famous sketchbook," said Santo, "if you happen to have it with you."

"It's right here," I said, pulling it out of my backpack.

Santo sat down with my sketchbook on his lap. He adjusted his glasses and spent several minutes looking carefully at the drawings and notes on each page before turning to the next. I'm pretty sure I stopped breathing.

"I think you and your sketchbook landed in just the right place," he said, signing a page for me. "Just know that if this is what you want to do, it's a long road. You're lucky to be working with some of the most talented and amazing people, but they've all worked incredibly hard for a long time."

"I can't believe I met Santo," I said over and over on the trolley ride back. "I mean, I really can't believe it."

"Well, you did," Marjory said, laughing. "Believe it."

"I can't believe it. And I can't believe he looked at my sketchbook."

"Well, he did," said Marjory. "Believe it."

"Do you realize that none of these things would have happened if you hadn't been the person to find my sketchbook?" I said.

"Well, lucky for both of us, I did," said Marjory.

When we got back to the wardrobe department, Marjory went to her office, where the message light on her phone was blinking like crazy. No sooner had she sat down than one person after another filed in to tell her about new problems that had cropped up.

"If we choose this fabric, it will cost twice as much . . ."

"Two of the sewing machines just broke . . ."

"Now they need the rest of the *Giselle* costumes a week earlier . . ."

I left the wardrobe department that afternoon exhausted just from watching Marjory manage so many different projects at once. I hadn't liked it when Verity corrected Enid and said I was an apprentice or that I needed to be able to sew to make costumes or fashion. But I began to realize that she was right. Watching Leticia Blum and Austin Tornado yell at people on *Off the Rack* was fun, but even the people on television knew a lot more than I did.

"Guess what," I said to Verity when I saw her.

"What?" she asked suspiciously.

"You won't believe who I met today."

FROM HEAD . . .

"We are very lucky that everyone who works with the costumes and sets are together in the same building," Marjory
explained to me the next week. "In smaller companies you
often work with outside milliners and wigmakers, and it
makes it a little more complicated, with more meetings and
fittings.

"Heads up, everyone," Marjory called as we walked to the
back of the workroom, where two smaller rooms were blocked
off by a wall with a large glass window.

"Pippa, meet Stephen and Elizabeth, our milliners. These

are the people who are responsible for the nearly three hundred and forty headpieces we use in *Sleeping Beauty.*"

Elizabeth said, "We make crowns, hats, tiaras, fancy headpieces, feathered plumes . . ."

"As you can see, we don't have a lot of space in here," said Stephen, gesturing toward the shelves lined with Styrofoam heads. There were cabinets with wires and decorations spilling out of drawers and partially finished headpieces on tables and chairs. Pegboards hung on the walls with tools and glue guns dangling from hooks.

The back room was where all the decorations were kept in drawers and boxes. It was like the stitchers' cabinet had multiplied.

"Everyone calls us the Mad Hatters," said Stephen, "like in *Alice in Wonderland*. Only in our case, we have to make the hats."

"Here's a bit of real history," said Elizabeth. "In the fifteenth century, a milliner meant someone who sold hats, but by the eighteenth century it referred to the city of Milan in Italy, which became famous for making straw hats."

The milliners work in pretty much the same way as everyone else in the wardrobe department: by starting with the designer's sketches and doing lots of research and then figuring out how to make the headgear.

"No one's head is shaped exactly the same way," said Stephen. "Even the place where the ears are positioned is different on each person, which is why we have to make so many individual headpieces. For crowd scenes we can reuse hats and some of the headpieces."

"Since we can't keep people's heads, we work off these different-size models of heads, called *poupees* (pronounced *pu-peys*)," said Elizabeth, "and make samples called toiles."

A poupee with a toile on top

"First we have to work out the form of the headpiece, usually by bending and playing with thin wire. Later we'll add some layers of netting and fabric so we can sew on the decorations."

Elizabeth made a fascinator for me, which a lot of fancy ladies wear to formal events. It's a light headpiece decorated with feathers, flowers, and beads that is attached to a clip or a comb.

"The designer gives us a sketch or some direction about the headpieces," said Stephen. "We do research to help develop the idea into something that works for the character and the costume."

"For Carabosse, we were inspired by *hennins*, which are headpieces from the medieval period that are shaped like cones," explained Elizabeth. "Now there's one more person and place you need to see just down the hall."

A variety of headpieces from *The Sleeping Beauty*

Wig room at the National Ballet of Canada

I didn't mind the Styrofoam heads the milliners used, but there was something a little strange about seeing rows of Styrofoam heads wearing different hairstyles.

"Don't wig out," said a friendly-looking man named Charlie. He was pulling strands of hair through a metallic mesh skullcap. "It's just like hooking a rug," he said, knotting a strand of hair through one of the tiny openings. "We use mostly human hair for the wigs and add a layer of horsehair to the cap part so we can pin it to the dancer's real hair."

"How long does it take to make a wig?" I asked.

"Anywhere from six to nine days," said Charlie. "You can

CHARLIE

buy commercial wigs and rework them, but they don't last as long. If you're working with a wig, you have to think about whether the headpiece will sit on top of the head or if it will use lace or gold braid that falls over the forehead.

"One reason we have so many wigs in *Sleeping Beauty* is because Louis XIV wanted to hide the fact that he was going bald, so he made it popular to wear what were called *periwigs*. Of course, no one's wig was styled exactly the same way, so we have an assortment of different hairstyles. Back in the seventeenth century, unlike now, no one really washed their wigs. It was common for them to get bugs and other unpleasant things."

I squirmed a bit, remembering Verity's legwarmers.

"It was very nice to meet you," I said to Charlie before I left for the day.

"Hair's hoping I'll see you again, Pippa," he replied.

. . . TO TOE

If the Lilac Fairy was real and ran a small business grant-
ing wishes, Verity would ask for pointe shoes. The supers are
always talking about when their feet will be strong enough
to go en pointe, which is when a dancer balances their full
weight on the tips of their toes.

Getting your first pair of pointe shoes is a very big deal,
but Verity has ruined all the magic for me with some truly
disgusting descriptions about the icky things that can happen
to dancers' feet.

The next Wednesday, Verity popped into the wardrobe

room and announced that she was getting measured for her *Sleeping Beauty* slippers just loudly enough for everyone, including Marjory, to hear.

"Do you get pajamas, too?" I asked.

Verity rolled her eyes, but before she could say anything, Marjory said, "Pippa, you should go to the shoe room. Your costume education wouldn't be complete without it, and you'll get a chance to meet Lorna."

Lorna is a legend around here. She started as a student and was invited to join the company and perform all over the world. Marjory told me that Lorna has three different jobs: 1) principal character artist; 2) assistant ballet mistress, which is like a coach and advisor to the younger dancers in the company; and 3) pointe shoe manager.

We took the elevator down to the first floor and found the shoe room, which is actually three rooms that open up into one another.

Lorna finished saying goodbye to another dancer and then came over to us. "Welcome," she said in a friendly voice.

Verity was gaping at the floor-to-ceiling cubbies filled with pointe shoes. She turned to Lorna, looking like someone who had walked into a magical kingdom made of pink satin.

"There must be a million shoes in here," I said.

"More like five thousand," said Lorna. "That's because pointe shoes don't last through more than eight hours of wear. Many of our dancers go through one pair for each performance, which can add up to between sixty and eighty shoes a year per dancer."

Ballet shoes upon ballet shoes!

"But right now," Lorna said, guiding Verity toward a bench, "I need to make sure *this* dancer is fitted properly for her ballet shoes."

Verity got her feet measured: length, width, height of instep, and arch.

Ballet slippers are supposed to fit snugly like a glove but still have enough room for toes to move.

These are the kind of ballet shoes Verity wears:

- made of canvas
- split sole
- a bit of suede leather on heel and ball of the foot—allows dancer to emphasize the arch of the foot by pointing her toes
- come in white, black, and flesh colors, but can be dyed any color

An up-close view of pointe shoes

"I bet Marie Taglioni would have liked to wear pointe shoes instead of slippers," I said.

"A ballet historian," said Lorna, looking impressed.

My comment snapped Verity out of her trance long enough to shoot me a look for showing off.

"After Taglioni, more dancers began performing en pointe, but their technique was limited since slippers didn't provide any protection," said Lorna.

Verity was rising up and down on her feet for Lorna but quickly asked, "How are pointe shoes made now?"

"The shoemaker uses a mold of the dancer's foot and then places layers of glue and canvas over the mold to make the toe area into a kind of box that supports the foot. The shoe is then hardened in a very hot oven and finally covered with colored satin. The sole of the shoe is made of hard leather, which prevents it from bending too freely and also helps to support the feet as the dancer moves up and down off their toes, like shock absorbers in a car.

"Pointe shoes are not sized like regular shoes but are adjusted in order to custom-fit every type of foot."

Toe Box

- square box in toe called a "block"
- ribbons are sewn on by hand
- elastic is sewn across the instep of the shoe, over the arch
- a cord hidden in a casing on the top opening of the shoe can be loosened or pulled tight as needed

"Now stand with your feet flat," said Lorna to Verity. "I need to see where your toes are so you don't slip." While she measured, Lorna continued, "I'm sure that by now you've seen dancers cutting, scraping, ripping, and sewing or gluing their shoes."

Verity nodded. "That's how they break in their shoes to make them fit perfectly."

"Well, there is nothing more important in a costume to a dancer than their shoes," said Lorna. "And, of course, you need pink tights or leg makeup that matches the shoes to give a dancer that long, elegant line."

When she was done with Verity's feet, Lorna showed us the room where the slippers and boots for the male dancers are kept.

"Men don't do pointe work, so they wear black slippers. But in *Sleeping Beauty*, Prince Florimund and the huntsmen have to wear boots. We have them custom-made," said Lorna.

Ballet Boot

- no heel
- completely conform to dancer's feet

- zipper up the inside of the leg
- strong elasticized panels at the side, which are less lumpy
- painted with a matte paint to look like leather, in the color specified by the designer

Lorna told us about how once a dancer's shoe flew off the stage during a performance and how, in a different production, one of the ballerinas had to wear trousers, somehow got her shoe stuck in the bottom of her pant leg, and then had to hop offstage.

I definitely think Lorna could add storyteller as a fourth job.

Yet another type of ballet shoe: the ballet boot

"I look forward to measuring you for your first pair of pointe shoes one day," she told Verity.

"Thank you," Verity said with a smile.

"Thank you so much," I said. "This was the high pointe of our day."

VERITY HAS A FIT(TING) DAY

With tech week only a few days away and opening night one week later, the wardrobe department was in full swing with final costume fittings. I knew from Ruth that with such a large cast—the "Garland Waltz" alone has fifty-seven costumes—this was a big job.

"I'm afraid today will be more of a spectator sport," Marjory told me. "Are you up for handing us pins?"

"Well, we know one fitting that will be exciting today," said Ruth, giving me a wink.

I shivered a little with excitement thinking about the

surprise we had planned for Verity, who was scheduled to come in later this afternoon.

In the meantime, the fittings were like a revolving door of dancers going into the dressing room wearing their practice clothes or streetwear and emerging totally transformed by the beautiful costume they were wearing.

Then they stood on a small platform while Marjory, Ruth, and one of stitchers pinned straps, hooks, and fabric so that everything fit the dancer perfectly.

Marjory told me that one of the best parts about helping with fittings is getting to know the dancers a little better.

Sometimes she learns a few secrets, like the time a soloist told her he was planning to propose to another dancer who was scheduled for a fitting the same day. She had a very hard time keeping that quiet.

"Guess who's next?" Ruth said.

I could hardly look at Verity when she came in, but she was so excited to try on her costume that she wouldn't have noticed anything anyway.

Marjory held up a long blue dress with a tight bodice. The bodice ended in a V-point over a full skirt with layers of fabric that fell in tiers like frosting on a cake.

The oval neckline had a band of lace, and the sleeves were full with some serious ruffles at the wrist.

Verity gasped when she saw it. "It's so beautiful," she repeated over and over.

"Ruth will help you put this on," said Marjory. "But before you change, just look inside."

Verity peered inside the costume and let out a squeal when she saw the label sewn inside had her name.

"It was Pippa's idea," said Marjory. "And since this is a new costume, your name will be the first one written inside."

"Thank you!" said Verity. "This is so special. I'll always remember this."

Verity came out of the dressing room looking like someone who had stepped out of a fairy tale. Holding her skirts
up, she walked carefully to the platform, where Ruth pulled
in some of the fabric around her waist.

Verity was still swishing and turning in front of the mirror when a group of three dancers arrived. One with her hair
in a bun called out, "Wow, Verity, I hardly recognized you.
You really look like you're from another century."

"I *feel* like I'm from another century," said Verity, who looked somewhat awed that this dancer was speaking to her.

She took one more look at herself in the mirror and quickly scampered down to go and change.

"This is one of our Auroras," said Marjory as the ballerina with the bun came over for her fitting.

That explained why Verity looked so starstruck.

"Hey, I recognize you," said one of the other dancers, who was wearing regular jeans and a ponytail. "You were the sketchbook girl with the fashion designs."

Aurora had replaced Verity on the platform and was trying on the costume for act 2.

"Good thing this is so pretty," she joked, "since I have to wear it for a hundred years." Then she looked at me and asked, "Have these magicians convinced you to become a costume designer instead?"

"She may not have to choose," said Marjory. "Don't forget that ballet and fashion have influenced each other and that there are many fashion designers who have worked on ballets, including the great Coco Chanel. Jeanne Lanvin, Ralph Rucci, Karl Lagerfeld, Valentino, and Rodarte's Mulleavy

Robe de Style dress designed by Jeanne Lanvin
(French, 1867–1946), fall/winter 1926

sisters, just to name a few, have all been invited by ballet companies to create costumes."

"Then there's Christian Lacroix," said a stitcher who had come over to help Ruth. "He's both a fashion and costume designer, but when you look at some of his collections and the way he uses frills, sparkles, and embroidery, you can tell they are inspired by ballet. His puffball skirt even mimics the shape of a tutu."

Dress costume designed by Paul Poiret
(French, 1879–1944), 1911

"In 1910 the artist Léon Bakst designed harem pants and turbans for the ballet *Scheherazade,* which had an *Arabian Nights* theme. A couturier named Paul Poiret turned the harem pants into a suit in his collection, and they were wildly popular," added Ruth.

Verity had returned from changing and was watching Ruth carefully hang her costume on one of the racks.

"I'll be really careful when I wear it," she said to Ruth. "I don't want anything to happen to it."

"I remember one time," said Aurora, "when a dancer did a backbend and got her tiara stuck in her skirt."

UNRAVELING
COSTUME

FORGOT TO
take OFF her leg warmers!

A HANGER
Still on her Back!

Verity looked horrified as this story set off more stage-disaster stories:

The dancer who stepped on his partner's costume and tore it so badly that it began to unravel.

The dancer who wore a beautiful costume but forgot to take off her warmup socks.

The dancer who came out onstage and still had the hanger in her costume.

"Stop," said Verity, who had always been a little superstitious. "We don't want to bring on any disasters."

"Don't fret," said the Aurora dancer, chucking Verity under her chin. "Those dancers didn't have Marjory and Ruth and this wardrobe department behind them. Nothing will go wrong."

IF IT CAN GO WRONG, IT WILL GO WRONG

Verity had a rehearsal on Friday, so I went to the fourth floor to work in Marjory's office, copying the last few pages I needed from the bible into my sketchbook.

When Marjory came into her office to check for messages, she told me that a lot of bad things had happened this week.

A dancer got injured and had to be replaced, which meant adding more fittings to the schedule. The fabric for the huntsmen costumes never arrived, so Chris had to run to a fabric store to find something else. A headpiece that had taken

weeks to make had been broken. Lily came down with the flu
and had to leave early.

It made me wonder if Verity had been right to worry.

"You'll have to come with us to rehearsal," Mom said the
next day. "Dad has to go out, and Verity has to have one
parent there."

When we got to the ballet, Verity found out that they
weren't ready for her scene, so we decided to head up to the
fourth floor. I expected the wardrobe department to be a bit
frenzied, but I did not expect to find everyone in the workroom in a panicky state, carrying piles of papers and furniture
out of Marjory's office.

It turned out that a real disaster had occurred after everyone left the night before: A pipe broke on the floor above
Marjory's office. Water gushed through the ceiling, ruining
books, a bolt of expensive fabric, and the piles of photos and
papers on her desk.

Worst of all, the *Sleeping Beauty* bible was a giant mush
of wet, soggy paper.

"I don't know what we're going to do," said Marjory.
"After we clean this up, we'll meet in the kitchen and use
everyone's notes to try to reconstruct whatever we can."

"I can't believe this happened to the bible right before tech week," one of the cutters said.

"More like *wreck* week," said Chris.

"Pippa's been copying the bible into her sketchbook," said Verity.

Everyone turned to look at me.

"Is this true?" said Marjory.

"She even put in all the swatches and things you gave her," Verity chirped.

"Can I see?" asked Marjory.

"I thought it was okay to copy everything. Not that my sketches are very good. I just wanted to remember everything, and I—"

"Just. Stop. Talking," said Verity. "No one is mad at you."

I pulled my sketchbook out of my bag and handed it to Marjory. Everyone gathered around her as she began thumbing through the pages.

"Look, she's even got some of the swatches . . ."

"And the buttons . . ."

"Are those pattern pieces?"

"There's a copy of Prince Florimund's jacket."

"Oh my goodness," said Marjory. "I can't believe it."

"Believe it," I said jokingly, as everyone swooped around me in a giant hug.

I'll admit that I was a little nervous to leave my sketchbook *again*, especially after all the work I had done to track it down, but this time I knew it was in good hands with Marjory and the wardrobe department—and they promised to give it back as soon as they finished re-creating their bible.

It seemed so long ago that Verity had written the extra rehearsal dates for tech week on the calendar, and then, suddenly, it was here.

Super Saturday Sleepovers were suspended until *Sleeping Beauty* closed, but everyone including Mom was at the theater.

Behind the scenes, everything is just as choreographed and planned out as it is onstage. There's even a special crew called the running wardrobe department, which is in charge of handling the costumes during each night of the ballet.

Barbara is the head wardrobe coordinator and mistress who oversees the dressers—the people responsible for getting dancers into and out of their costumes. If you are a principal dancer, you have your own dresser. Company dancers share dressers, and supers get volunteer parents, like Mom.

Although I wouldn't be able to actually go backstage during a dress rehearsal or performance to see the running wardrobe department in action, Barbara gave me the rundown of how it all works.

Each dresser gets something called a *plot*, which is a list of each scene along with its costume changes. On the night of a performance, the schedule looks like this:

- **1 hour to curtain:** Dressers take first costumes, tights, and underwear to the appropriate dressing rooms.

- **30 minutes to curtain:** Dressers pre-set the costumes needed for quick changes on the side stage and make sure everything is in the right order for the right characters.

- **15 minutes to curtain:** Dressers return to the dressing rooms to help fasten, hook, and zip dancers into their first costumes.

- **Curtain Up:** Dressers move between the dressing rooms and side stage.

- **Curtain Down:** Dressers help dancers out of costumes, hang up costumes, and collect laundry.

I also found out that in addition to being a wigmaker, Charlie is one of the makeup artists. My favorite part of tech week was when he invited me to watch him work on the dancer playing Carabosse, who wears a skullcap that goes under her wig.

Charlie added one ugly hooked nose, two darkened eyebrows, dramatic eyeliner, and blackened teeth and lips. Then he used brushes and sponges to add layers of makeup until suddenly I was looking at one scary witch.

In the wardrobe department, everyone was working at full speed, and Marjory had even hired some extra stitchers to finish all the adjustments to the costumes in time. (No one wanted to repeat the style of the famous Karinska, who used to arrive with her stitchers in taxis and get dancers dressed minutes before they were supposed to go onstage.)

And then, suddenly, opening night had arrived.

OPENING NIGHT

Mom and Verity were getting ready to leave for the theater when Dad bellowed, "Everyone to the living room."

A large box wrapped in brown paper was sitting there with my name on it.

"Special delivery for Pippa," said Dad.

"I feel like this has happened before," joked Mom.

"Open it," said Verity, bouncing up and down on her toes.

Inside was a shimmery silver dress. Something about it looked familiar, but I couldn't figure it out.

"Do you recognize it?" asked Verity. "Look at the back."

I looked and saw a row of pearl buttons. I realized it was one of my own designs!

"You aren't the only one to plan a surprise, Pippa," said Mom.

"Even that horrible Banquette would be impressed," said Dad.

"Put it on before we leave," said Verity.

Even without being measured, the dress fit perfectly.

"But how did you even do this?" I asked.

Verity smiled slyly. "Fairies helped me," she said.

Even though there are still so many things I have to learn about costumes, I do know that sometimes my sister can be pretty great.

"My goodness," said Mom.

I felt very glamorous when Dad and I arrived at the theater. I couldn't stop swishing the full skirt of my dress around.

The musicians were warming up, and ushers were helping people find their seats. Verity's name was in the program, and I was surprised to see that I was included with the rest of the wardrobe department as a "special apprentice."

Finally the performance started, and for the first time I could see how the costumes and sets and dancing all came together on the stage.

At intermission, I heard a lady sitting behind us say, "I can't imagine how they make those spectacular costumes."

PIPPA

opening night

I thought back to everything that had happened. How an idea became a drawing, and bolts of fabric went from one set of hands to another and ended with the visions of tulle and silks and sparkles that flew across the stage.

It really was magic.

At the end of the performance, someone came out from backstage and presented Princess Aurora with a ginormous bouquet of flowers while everyone applauded.

She curtsied three times and then motioned for everyone to stop clapping as she moved closer to a microphone that had been placed on the stage.

"There is someone we would like to invite to the stage, someone who has become something of a star herself in the wardrobe department," she announced. "Would Pippa please come up?"

There's no way I could ever be a dancer with the way my legs were shaking as I walked up to the side of the stage and climbed the stairs to join Princess Aurora and the rest of the company.

Prince Florimund stepped forward and, with a very elaborate bow, handed me a beautiful little bouquet of flowers.

Princess Aurora gave me a kiss and then the Lilac Fairy tiptoed up to hand me my sketchbook.

Then Princess Aurora, Prince Florimund, the Lilac Fairy, Carabosse, and I took our final bow.

As for my sketchbook . . . well, inside I found this message:

Dear Pippa,

After all this time you have a whole department of not-so-secret admirers! Thank you for lending us your sketchbook. We noticed there are a few pages left to be filled. Perhaps you'll save your Wednesdays for some more adventures in the Wardrobe Department next season.

xoxo

Marjory Ruth Elizabeth
CHRIS Lily LISA
Stephen Charlie
LORNA Cece IDA

Photo Credits

Acknowledgments

I am indebted to two extraordinary women: The real Marjory Fielding from the Wardrobe Department of the National Ballet of Canada for giving me the experience and friendship of a lifetime.

And to the late-legendary Frances Foster who was in every way an inimitable and irreplaceable one-of-a-kind editor and an unparalleled human being. You are with me every day.

At the National Ballet of Canada: huge thanks to the wardrobe wonders: Ruth, Chris, Charlie, Victoria, Lisa, Lorna, Barb, and everyone else who so generously shared their remarkable talents and expertise for this book.

Special thanks to Santo Loquasto for the generous use of his sketches.

To Valerie Steele, Director of Museum at FIT, for giving me the benefit of her vast knowledge.

NYCB Wardrobe Supervisor Marc Happel.

Holly Hynes.

Connie Coburn: the chicest archivist and best possible friend.

Karen Klockner: a magician and wonderful friend who was there the whole time.

And finally, my own indispensable corps de famille, who are everything: Chris, Ben, and Otti.

Now would someone please take the poodles out for a walk.

BACKSTAGE NOTES

The importance of costumes in a performance goes beyond the visual impression they make—especially in ballet, where movement takes the place of spoken words.

Costumes transform dancers into characters. They are part of why we allow ourselves to believe that for the time we sit in our seats, we are in a different time and place.

There is another story that the audience does not see. It is hidden in the silver button sewn on the cuff of a sleeve, or the ribbon and sparkling beads on a gown—so small that they are almost invisible to even those in the front row.

They are important details, parts that help create a whole, created by a team of talented artists who work in the wardrobe department.

It is here that bolts of fabric, spools of thread, wires, and vats of dye are turned into a ball gown, a cat, or a witch.

I was fortunate enough to spend time with the people I

have come to think of as magicians at the National Ballet of Canada's wardrobe department in Toronto, Canada.

This was the setting for *Pippa*, and while she is a fictional character, everything you and she learn and see is exactly what happens.

Welcome to the backstage world of ballet costumes.

Museums

These are just a few of the many museums with costume collections that you can visit . . .

- Metropolitan Museum of New York/Anna Wintour Costume Center, New York
- Museum at FIT and Archives, New York
- Victoria and Albert Museum, London, United Kingdom
- Fashion Museum Bath, Bath, United Kingdom
- Los Angeles County Museum of Art, Los Angeles
- Powerhouse Museum, Sydney, Australia
- McCord Museum, Montreal, Canada
- Palais Galliera (formerly known as the Musée de la Moda de la Ville de Paris), Paris, France
- National Gallery of Victoria, Melbourne, Australia
- National Museum of Dance and Hall of Fame, Saratoga Springs, New York